The patterns on Foundry Editions' covers have been designed to capture the visual heritage of the Mediterranean. This one is inspired by representations of the sea in Islamic miniature paintings. It was created by Hélène Marchal.

ABDEL AZIZ BARAKA SAKIN is one of the most prominent writers from Sudan today. He was born in Kassala, eastern Sudan, in 1963 and lived in Khashm el-Girba until he was forced into exile by the Islamist military regime in Khartoum. Most of his major works are banned in his home country, but his books are secretly traded and circulated online among Sudanese readers of all generations. Sakin's work *al-Jungo Masameer al-Ardh*, which appeared in English as *The Jungo: Stakes of the Earth*, was the winner of Tayeb Salih's Novel Award. Sakin lives in Austria and writes for a number of prominent Arab literary publications such *al-Arabi*, the London-based *al-Dastoor* newspaper, and *Al Jazeera* online.

MAYADA IBRAHIM is a literary translator based in Queens, New York, with roots in Khartoum and London. She works between Arabic and English. Her translations have been nominated for the Pushcart Prize and published by Willows House in South Sudan, Archipelago Books, Dolce Stil Criollo, and 128 Lit. She is the managing editor at Tilted Axis Press.

ADIL BABIKIR is a Sudanese translator into and out of English and Arabic, living in Abu Dhabi. He has translated *Mansi: A Rare Man in His Own Way* by Tayeb Salih (Banipal Books, 2020), *Modern Sudanese Poetry: An Anthology* (University of Nebraska Press, 2019), *The Beauty Hunters: Sudanese Bedouin Poetry, Evolution and Impact* (University of Nebraska Press, 2023), and several novels and short stories by renowned Sudanese writers.

SAMAHANI

ABDELAZIZ BARAKA SAKIN

Samahani

Translation by Mayada Ibrahim and Adil Babikir

FOUNDRY
EDITIONS

Nothing can stand in a lover's way.

SWAHILI PROVERB

Evil should be combated with the weapons of Goodness and Love. When it is Love that destroys an evil, this evil is killed forever. Brute force only temporarily buries the evil that it wants to combat and destroy. Now, evil is a persistent seed. Once buried, it develops in secret, germinates, and reappears with even greater vigor.

TIERNO BOKAR,
A FULANI MYSTIC FROM BANDIAGARA,
ADVISING HIS STUDENT AMADOU HAMPÂTÉ BÂ

What right have you to enslave those who were born free?

UMAR IBN AL-KHATTAB

BETWEEN HEAVEN AND HELL

Harut fixed the Blessed Sultan's age at exactly fifty-four years, two months, one week, three days and five hours. Harut was the Torahic name bestowed upon the sorcerer by Sultan Suleiman bin Salim himself, in honour of the legendary angels and master sorcerers Harut and Marut. Fixing the sultan's age at fifty-four years, two months, one week, three days, and five hours was significant, according to Harut, because it was Satan's age when he disobeyed the divine order to bow down to the creature God had created from clay taken from a swamp in heaven, the creature who came to be known as "Adam" in some quarters and elsewhere as "the human being". Satan, who was created from fire, reasoned that Adam was created from a vastly inferior element. Needless to say, Satan is the grand master of all magic orders on earth and later in the netherworld, as revealed in the book of *al-Juljulūtiyya al-Kubra*, and in manuscripts written in Geʻez and found in ancient caves on the Ethiopian plateau, near the city of Gondar.

At least according to those knowledgeable in the Secret Codes, the sultan could live five times the age written for him in the Preserved Tablet when he was still just a cell in his mother's womb, a mere thought in God's mind. This was to remain a secret known only to the sultan. He was never to disclose his real age, be it in conversation or in written form. He was to sow constant doubt among his subjects about his age. It is important to mention this at the outset, as the novel delves into the story of the Blessed Sultan, eternal ruler of the islands of Unguja and Bimba and the surrounding isles, self-proclaimed commander of all that is in the heavens, except God of course, and all that is on earth, except China, since it's too far away.

The narrator will now turn to the setting of the novel.

In 1652, immense ships hailing from Oman arrived at the coast of what was known during a murky period in history as Unguja. Zanzibar is its present-day Arabic name, derived from Zanj Barb, the Negro Coast, the name given to the island by a clattering of drunkard Persian sailors who happened upon it by chance some centuries ago. What they found were dark inhabitants, dense thickets of bushes, wild animals, trees laden with ripe fruit, and a species of bloodsucking nocturnal flies known today as mosquitoes. For one reason or another, they did not take to Zanzibar and returned to Persia, and because the barriers of language and fear were impenetrable on both sides, they took nothing with them except tales they had fabricated and come to believe about the land and its people, and they left nothing behind except a single Persian word: Zanj Barb, which underwent a series of transformations across languages, encounters, and epochs before ultimately taking its current form.

On board the Omani ships were destitute soldiers, wayward merchants, and seamen on a one-way voyage. Their ship commander had told them as much.

Fight courageously and defeat the enemy, and you'll inherit this paradise with all its bliss and its black houris. Your mixed offspring may even return to Oman one day. But turn away like cowards, and you'll meet your end.

To the commander, the "enemy" was both the indigenous people, who were portrayed as cannibals and evil sorcerers by the early seamen, and the Portuguese, who occupied the African inland and the islands on the coast. The Portuguese were engaged in an earnest search for gold, silver, and diamonds, as they were wont to do. They hunted animals for precious skins and tusks, and gathered wild herbs for medicinal purposes and magic rituals. They spent their recreational time in the company of curvaceous black women, as well as those who lacked such features, playing cards, drinking liquor distilled from dates, spreading the message of Christ, the Heavenly Father, or picking one-sided skirmishes with bothersome locals who invariably ended up killed or enslaved.

The Arab Omani army stunned the locals and Portuguese alike with its valour, its size, and its extensive arsenal. The Portuguese retreated inland to what was to become Angola, leaving the coastal area to the Arabs, who were armed with a highly destructive weapon: an awareness that they could not go back to where they had come from. This was the same weapon that had once enabled the Amazigh Tariq ibn Ziyad to occupy the Iberian Peninsula. As for the indigenous Africans, they were the hay that fed the fire for the Omanis to enjoy the abundance of their promised paradise, Unguja.

Here the reader may wish to consult the following passage from the memoir of Salma bint Saeed, daughter of one of the most legendary sultans from Hadhramaut to rule Zanjibar. Salma – or Emile Ruete, as she later came to be known in Germany – escaped her father's palace in 1867 with the German merchant Heidrich Ruete, whom she married and settled with in Berlin. This memoir is one of the dubious sources used in putting together this novel. Of course, the reader is at liberty to proceed directly to the first chapter.

> Another incident affecting the Arabs' sense of pride. A neighbour to the French consul chastised his recalcitrant slave as severely as he deserved, but, with a Negro's usual cowardice and inability to bear pain in silence, he struck up a frightful howl, which brought down the French consul's rather arrogant interference. This gentleman was himself no immaculate saint, seeming to hold the maxim, "let others practise what I preach." For he lived with a negress he had bought, who had presented to him an

excessively black little daughter – finally taken in by the French mission. It should cause no surprise if upon such experiences the Arabs distrust Europeans... "One ought to mind one's own business and not interfere in the affairs of strangers," he told him curtly.

> *Memoirs of an Arab Princess, translated by Salma Saleh, Dar al-Jamal, p. 267*

Those who read the foregoing paragraph may also wish to read an excerpt from *An Omani Adventurer in the African Jungles*, the biography of Hamad ibn Mohammed ibn Jum'a al-Marjabi, a fierce military leader who was born in 1840 and died of malaria in 1905. He was better known as Tippu Tip, a name mimicking the sound of bullets. The Africans also knew him as the Spotted Hyena. The novel makes only occasional references to him, and the reader may notice that historical accounts surrounding him and others are far from accurate, as the novel is ultimately concerned with the human rather than with history.

> Before dawn, our men went to inspect the dead among the enemy. There were more than 600 of them, their arrows, bows, drums and axes scattered around them. They clustered together and that hastened their demise. We remained there a long time. At around two in the morning, the enemy reappeared. We were ready for them but we waited until they came close to their hideout. Then we opened fire. In less than seven minutes, they fled, leaving

behind 150 dead. We lost only two. After chasing them for two hours, we returned to our camp.

An Omani Adventurer in the African Jungles, translated by Mohammed al-Mahrooqi, Dar al-Jamal, p. 51

A YOUNG WOMAN IN LOVE

The Blessed Princess loved the scents of the marketplace, particularly the fermented coconut when the breeze mixed it with the scent of cloves, fresh ginger, and lemon, and carried it to her delicate nose. She loved the colours of mangoes: rich yellow, green, gold, pink. They reminded her of her childhood of endless frolicking. They also reminded her of the strange discoloration on her growing breasts. The princess could trace each scent back to the kiosk it came from. The market was divided into eastern and western sections, with vegetable kiosks on one side and perfumes and oils on the other, ending at the slave market. But it was the smell of burning sulphur she could not help but follow to the kiosk of the Indian goldsmith.

Since her revelling husband had agreed to sever his relations with all his concubines – the Romanian, the two Ethiopians, the voluptuous Ungujan, the mercurial Copt, the Indians with the perky breasts who never stopped talking, the strange Sicilian recently bought from Oman, who some suspect is a jinn because an old Omani slaver claimed to have captured her from the Indian Ocean – she had developed an obsession with spending the money he had sold them for to buy all the jewellery she could get her hands on.

She fantasised about making them drink her urine, so deep was her hatred for them.

Whores. Vulgar thighs of all colours filling the house with their clamour.

Her ultimate aim was to lure her husband; not because she loved him but because she wanted to captivate him, to overpower him, knowing perfectly well that he loved nothing but the throne.

He can wait all he wants. My father won't die any time soon.

The princess loved the din of the market: the pedlars' cries, the slavers' auction bells, the call to prayer, the braying of donkeys, the hammering of ironsmiths, the shrieking of saws on wood, the roaring of mills operated by heavyset slaves whose hands grew sore and cracked, the bleating of goats being led to slaughter. But her favourite sound was that of the young Unguja singer Uhuru, which she preferred even to the ensemble her father had sent to Egypt for training and whose music she found odd and lifeless. She loved Uhuru's songs. Uhuru was the only free negro on Unguja, save for the old people begging and picking rotten fruit and vegetables off the streets, emancipated only once they became a burden on their masters: too old to work and in need of care.

She loved the discordant rhythm of Uhuru's three-legged drum. From behind her diaphanous veil, the princess cast covetous, envious glances at her naked breasts, which Uhuru carelessly displayed like forbidden fruit tainted by darkness. No one dared touch her, no human nor jinn, not even the princess's reckless husband. The singer often stood at the corner between the slave and gold market where the turbaned goldsmiths sat, their heads full of numbers and one-liners to draw money out of purses. She wore a goat-skin loincloth and sang "My Homeland is Heaven for the Occupiers and Hell for the Natives". The princess found the song somewhat hostile; or rather it made her feel a tinge of shame. She preferred the rhythm of another, far more brutal song, which described the day slavers had attacked Uhuru's village. Uhuru had memorised it in her native Swahili, spoken in the dialect of the Kaimondi tribe.

> As I was hiding among the trees
> The slavers came to Nyamwezi
> From my post, I watched them leave
>
> In the house were women galore
> A bad man came, and then one more
> Forced one to bed, forced them all
>
> The only one left behind
> Was the woman heavy with child

As Uhuru started to dance, Sondus, the castrated slave and the princess's personal servant, urged on the donkey that carried the princess, who sat majestically in a flowing Wakingo gown, drenched in glittering jewels, like a Kushite queen of King Solomon's era. The princess did not neglect to throw a handful of Maria Theresa thalers for Uhuru, taking care to keep her distance, for it was widely believed that anyone who came into physical contact with Uhuru would be struck by black magic. This was one of the reasons the slave hunters, who only saw people in terms of their market value, stayed clear of her. Uhuru picked up the coins hastily and put them in a secret pocket inside her tattered loincloth. "Asante sana," she said.

The princess hated the way Uhuru lost herself when she danced, exposing even her genitals and drawing out the most despicable men: bleary-eyed, drunk old fools who believed seeing a woman's sex improved their eyesight. She spun out of control, like a crazed dervish or an animal in the midst of attack.

She acts this way so no one dares go near her. I can't stand it.

The myth Uhuru had invented protected her from merchants and insatiable men, fuelled by their excessive intake of ginger and cloves, who took advantage of a law and social order that encouraged them to own for pleasure as many women and young boys as they liked.

The myth went as follows:

A mighty, faceless jinn will latch on to anyone who dares

touch me. No one banish it, not even the most renowned sorcerers who fast all year and live in caves at the edge of the world.

I dare them to try.

I dare them to try to sell me to the ships bound for the land of the whites.

I dare them to untie the goatskin round my waist.

I will dance the devil's dance, the devil you fear like nothing else, the devil that will consume your souls as swiftly as fire consumes dry grass.

With a little wickedness and some brazen lies, she protected her freedom.

Qaroon, the Indian goldsmith, was a crafty man. His namesake was a figure in the Quran known for his avarice. Qaroon was generous only when it was guaranteed he would receive his due in multiples. He waited for the princess, as he always did on the first Saturday of the lunar month. It was the day ships coming from the west lay anchor, delivering the most coveted merchandise.

The jewellery shop was small but well-equipped. In a remote corner, a servant sat on the ground behind the forge blower. A brawny young man with a thick head of hair, his naked torso exposed a broad, hairless chest buried under layers of ash and dirt. His lower half was wrapped in a filthy leather cloth. He worked silently, occasionally scanning the room with his bulging eyes. He noticed Sondus, soft and clean, wearing silk and two large golden earrings.

"Look at that pampered eunuch! And look at *me*! A big mass of flesh, dark and filthy." The servant was chained to a steel wedge so deeply embedded in the ground that not even the mightiest elephant would be able to loosen it.

Inside the shop were small safes firmly placed on steel shelves, and oil paintings of Indian deities. A dancing Shiva faced the entrance. A chapter from the Holy Quran, "Surah Al-Falaq", transcribed in gold ink, was framed and placed over a large wooden box. And right behind the goldsmith was the sultan's family tree. The law required all establishments and palaces to display it.

Qaroon couldn't wait to show the princess his new selection of rare jewels, procured especially for her and sent by the chief goldsmith of France. She knew he was not telling the truth but chose to believe him nevertheless. She needed his carefully woven lies to arouse the jealousy of her conceited friends, the daughters, wives, and concubines of landlords and rich slave traders and clove merchants. Better still if she could kill them with jealousy. She paid him far more than the tatty accessories were worth.

Out of a small gold-laminated box Qaroon pulled a small photograph of a white woman in a silk dress posing pompously. "Would you look at this precious necklace?" he said, pointing with a finger at a big gold ring adorned with a big diamond – a real diamond, he assured her. "It belongs to Duchess Mariana von Padova, the most enchanting of them all. I'm sure you've heard of her."

"I haven't."

"She is the most glamorous star in Italy," Qaroon said, with the photograph gently resting on his palm. "She captured the hearts of Italian and English poets alike. They have written volume upon volume in praise of her beauty. There's a shanty you hear seamen singing around here that was composed for her."

"Really?" she said, urging him to continue.

Like a seasoned burglar, the goldsmith sent his fingers rummaging inside the box and pulled out a glittering necklace. He swung it closer to the transparent veil. "A rare ruby piece. It adorned the great Duchess Mariana. And this in the middle is a black diamond – rarer than hen's teeth."

"How did you get your hands on it?" She reached out to examine it.

"The pirates!" he cried. His smile exposed yellow, decaying teeth. "The pirates, Your Highness, can acquire anything. My people in India believe the pirates created the oceans. Getting their hands on the necklace of Duchess Mariana is nothing to them." He laughed.

Even Qaroon's servant, sitting behind his forge blower, could see the princess's white teeth glitter behind the veil. Eyeing the necklace, blood rushed through her veins. Her heart beat faster; she could barely contain herself. The smell of burning sulphur stirred an irresistible lust for buying. The Indian gods and Quranic verses hanging on the wall seemed to tremble under Qaroon's thunderous laugh.

"It costs one thousand Maria Theresa thalers," said the goldsmith.

"How much?" she said, taken aback.

"Only a thousand Maria Theresa thalers," he replied, a little smile curving his lips. "A very special price for a very special client."

The necklace is divine, but I'm not paying a thousand for lies he made up.

"Five hundred. Nothing more," she said, rising from her chair.

A pause.

"Give him two hundred and fifty," she said to Sondus, who was stirring the stagnant air with a palm frond fan and swatting flies away from her gown.

"Didn't you just say five hundred?" asked Qaroon in a panic.

"Give him one hundred," she ordered.

Sondus continued to wave the fan.

"Your Highness, this is unfair."

"Give him fifty and nothing else."

Sondus started to pull out the coins from an old leather bag, selecting the ones with eroded edges. Qaroon counted them silently several times before placing them in a large box. Then he put the necklace in a small box and handed it over to the princess, who thanked him and left, trying with difficulty to suppress a laugh.

Qaroon slumped onto his seat and, in an outburst of pique, started tearing the photograph of the European model. Startled by sniggering coming from inside the kiosk, he threw a furious glance at the dark, shackled mass of flesh by the forge blower. Before leaving at the end of the day, old Qaroon made sure to use the hot solder to cast two new lines on his back, which had already come to resemble a worn fishing net.

FATHER, MASTER

"I am the sultan and I reign over everything on this island – the land, the plants, the animals, the seas, the ships, the boats, the catch, the hunters. The rivers, the flies, the mosquitoes, the ants, the rocks, the beaches, the deserts, and the jungles. Every bird, falcon, eagle, swan, and fox. I am the ultimate and eternal master. Even the sky overlooking the island is mine, and the wind that sweeps through it. The rain, storms, thunder, and lightning. Every man, woman, child, and slave. Every jinn and every angel. I made this paradise with my own hands. *I* am mine!" he brayed.

Thinking of the British, who had been trying to weaken his authority, he feebly added, "The English are mine too. The Germans, the French, the belligerent Belgians. The sea, the land, the mountains..."

He pointed his index finger at Mutei. "And you are mine too."

His dedicated servant Mutei was always by his side, awaiting orders, and when there were no orders he swatted away insects and listened intently to every word uttered by his master, interpreted every look, every movement. Occasionally the sultan lapsed into complete silence, leaving it to others to discern his unspoken desires and fulfil them promptly or suffer the consequences. Mutei was unperturbed by his master's outbursts, and he was accustomed to his strange questions, always responding with "Yes, Your Blessed Majesty."

Soon after Sultan Suleiman bin Salim coerced the island's leading religious scholar into creating a family tree that linked his lineage to King Solomon, master of humankind and jinn, he issued a decree ordering all his subjects to address him as "Your Blessed Majesty" and his daughter as "the Blessed Princess". His daughter Lateefa was nicknamed Fatuma in remembrance of her mother, Fatuma Jama, the only one among his ninety-nine women whose name he never forgot. A minority on the island secretly added an extra couple of words to the title of the sultan and his daughter, calling them "the recently blessed", given that the lineage to the Prophet Solomon had only emerged in the last few years.

It was common knowledge that the sultan hailed from Abyssinia, which had occupied Yemen for many decades, resulting in a distinct blend of civilisations and a beautiful language still used in both regions to this day.

It was evident to Mutei, looking at the sultan in his bed, that a difficult day lay ahead.

"You're a slave. You couldn't conceive of owning things you've always dreamt of, of having a big store of rials, treasures of gold and silver, hundreds of slaves, and a palace full of beautiful women and young men, the pleasure of owning everything on earth and everything in heaven, except God of course."

He farted, a signal for Mutei to fetch the tools and the rose water for cleaning. The sultan sat on a steel basin, a large receptacle specially made to accommodate him, since nothing else did. He often amused himself by posing riddles to Mutei that his grandmother had shared with him.

"A necklace at the top and red silver in the box."

Mutei stood motionless behind the sultan. He didn't know the answer. In any case, there was only one answer he was permitted to give.

"Yes, Your Blessed Majesty."

"I'm on my way, holding my ox by the tail."

"Yes, Your Blessed Majesty."

The foul smell began to engulf Mutei.

"My mother is carrying me. A coo here, a coo there, and a roaring lion inside."

A sound akin to a meow, followed by a ghastly odour.

"My hen laid eggs on the thorns. Right, now it's your turn – do it properly, you fool. Pour some sandalwood oil in the rose water. Make sure it's warm. How in the world would we have kept ourselves clean had God not created you? You are kind, but you are an imbecile. All you negroes are. There is a dimness to you. Well, no. Once I met a negro who strutted like a rooster, with his chest puffed out. His name was Simba. He was vicious, belligerent, and murderous. His poisonous arrows killed so many of our soldiers. He was very gifted at setting traps. Every time we thought we had escaped one, we found ourselves in another. We couldn't abduct even a single child from his village, and he captured all the elephant ivory and leopard skins that belonged to us. The only one to defeat him was the Spotted Hyena. After a year-long battle, they reached a truce. I don't need to tell you who the Spotted Hyena is. He chased you and your child out of the jungles and caves. He rescued you from a life of barbarism and cannibalism and from feeding on worms and wild boars. He led you to the light of civilisation, to Islam. Indeed, slaves can go to heaven, just like us, if they are good Muslims, if they cleanse themselves and give thanks to God. You should be thanking God, day and night, for the gift of living in this palace, and the gift of eating what a great sultan like me eats, a sultan from a long line of sultans, a descendant of Solomon."

His belly shook with laughter.

"Truth be told, you're a good servant. I can't know whether you will be rewarded with heaven or not, but I do know who will spend eternity in hell. Do you? Runaway slaves, that's who. Now do something about this hideous smell. It is beyond me why kings must defecate just like you do."

Mutei dried the sultan's rear with a linen towel, turning away in disgust from the hair and blemishes around his anus. He splashed what remained of the rose water with sandalwood oil. He then helped the sultan to stand on his old, plump legs.

Dibniba, who had later been given the name Mutei, was once a notable figure in his village on the western coast of Unguja, prior to being captured with his son Nano, later named Sondus. They had both been castrated in a brutal ceremony, the father in the presence of the son and the son in the presence of the unconscious father, babbling incoherently and biting down on a piece of wood that had been wedged into his mouth. The son lost the ability to speak. When his wounds began to heal, he was assigned to the service of the princess, who was close to him in age. The father was assigned to the sultan's service.

Perhaps father and son were chosen for their striking beauty. They were tall, with smooth, dark skin, broad eyes and full lips, and a quiet disposition. The masters preferred handsome machines that worked and did not talk, and a servant had to be able to keep a secret. Better still if they said nothing at all. Silence was an act of worship. As for other traits such as loyalty and honesty, these were acquired through skin-burning, flogging, solitary confinement, and denial of food and drink – acts alien to the African way of life. They choose mindless obedience, forsaking their human rights, but they keep dreaming all their lives of freedom, the way silent Sondus does.

Sultan Suleiman had two large palaces on the coast, and one in the countryside called Paradises that he modelled after his image of paradise. The women, whom he referred to as his houris, and the young men who belonged to him, lived there. His daughter's palace was built on a pebble beach on the western side of the island, in a somewhat remote area chosen for its spectacular nature and serenity, away from the hustle and bustle of the city that she happened to favour over the quiet.

The palaces reflected architectural styles of several civilisations across different continents: European, Indian, Yemeni, and Persian. The architects and masons had been summoned from all corners of the earth. The palaces were made of coral stone and limestone. The interior was predominantly oriental, with a touch of European and Islamic ostentatiousness.

Paradises Palace was the sultan's favourite; the other two were effectively administrative and residential units with hundreds of rooms inhabited by officials, workers, generals, and honourable guests such as merchants, politicians, and captains.

THE FATHER'S PALACE

Once the recently blessed sultan finished the ritual of relieving himself and purifying his body from the taint of carnal encounter, he prayed, reciting a few Quranic verses from memory. He only knew a handful of Arabic words, though he claimed to understand if spoken to, which was unlikely and perhaps simply reflected his longing for his native tongue.

With the sultan in the dining room, Mutei took the opportunity to retire to his private room in the servant quarters. He hadn't slept all night, as one of his duties was to minister to the sultan as he slept, even while women were present. It wasn't unusual to find a eunuch in the sultan's chamber while he engaged in intercourse. The sultan needed him there; he lived in fear of cunning women, imagining that one might poison him or smother him to death or put a spell on him, which was not unheard of. Although he had always depended on black magic, jinn, and even Satan himself over the course of his long life, he always said that "The cunning of women is greater than the power of jinn and demons. Their strength is second only to the strength of God, and God himself may respond to them while ignoring men." More importantly, since an injury to his left knee had left him unable to thrust his body with ease, he needed help penetrating the fuller women. It was necessary to have someone push down his enormous buttocks as he sprawled on top of them. This wasn't a problem when it came to the more slender houris, such as the Sicilian girl. In this case, Mutei assisted in guiding her motions as she rode atop the sultan. After spending much of the night attending to the sultan's needs, Mutei then had to guard the sultan as he slept, since women were permitted to enter his quarters at any time of day unless instructed otherwise.

The sultan set off for his weekly meeting with distinguished personages to resolve disputes and provide counsel on matters pertaining to daily life, faith, and governance. This was the task assigned to him since taking over from his father, who had defeated the Portuguese and chased them out of the island.

No one except the magician Harut knew the sultan's true age. His enemies estimated that he was more than a hundred years old. Yet he was sharp and physically fit, thanks to God first and to black magic second. The truth was that he relied on black magic more than he relied on God. He had been taught magic by an African slave whom he had rewarded with freedom, but the African had died in one of the attacks carried out by the Spotted Hyena, while the sultan lived on, likely for eternity.

On a luxurious seat in the courtyard, the sultan sat surrounded by his guests, who were placed in semicircles in order of status. Sitting on the front row were the renowned merchants, the princes' trusted friends, and the chief captain who oversaw all the vessels and managed maritime trade. They sat on low seats brought to them by the palace's servants. On the second row were wealthy locals on small wooden stools they had brought from their homes. The third row: immigrants who had recently arrived in search of new riches, and who could make their way to the front row once they had learned Swahili and acquired enough money, rank, and garments to be worthy of the council. This group usually sat on the ground or on palm branches. Finally, beggars and poor immigrants sat next to the elderly, the ill, the mentally disordered who were either released by their masters and left to fend for themselves in the middle of the city or dropped off by ships from unknown locations because they were no longer productive and their expiry date was fast approaching. Further away from the council, slaves looked after the masters' horses and donkeys. They fed them and separated the males from the females to avoid fighting. The slaves were not to address the council under any circumstances. That was only for their masters and owners to do. Besides, what could a slave possibly add if their master spoke on their behalf?

The council proceeded in as dull a manner as any other headed by Sultan Suleiman bin Salim. Until a blood-curdling scream was heard, coming from the heart of town, followed by gunfire. Moments later, soldiers on camels arrived at the palace and asked to speak to the sultan in private, but he urged them to spit it out.

"What's happened in town?"

"An attack by the barbaric negroes," replied a soldier, his chest heaving.

"Where did they come from?" snarled the sultan.

The soldier avoided the sultan's gaze. "We don't know. They were like hungry hyenas. They came down on the townspeople, robbed firearms from the armoury, and... they—"

"And what?" asked the sultan fearfully.

"The princess's palace—"

As if anticipating the news, the sultan quickly replied, "Where is she?"

"I'm afraid they took her with them," the soldier said, the rifle shaking in his grip.

"And what are you doing? Why haven't you wiped them out?" the sultan roared in disbelief.

"The townspeople are going after them. They slipped away, the cowards, but the townspeople are going after them, and they'll catch them. We came to let you know. We'll finish them off and bring back the princess and the stolen arms."

When the sultan's palm landed on the soldier's face, the court dispersed in a flash. Everyone hurtled towards town on donkeys and camels and on foot, with their slaves behind them. The blind, the elderly, the disabled, the beggars, all scuttled away. The sultan set about arbitrarily attacking the soldiers, kicking them with his fat, hairy legs, shouting, "Kill them all. Kill them, you cowards. Get out of my face. Kill them or I'll have you all killed."

The sultan hauled himself inside the palace. Mutei jumped out of bed and rushed towards his master, pushing past dozens of women, servants, cooks hiding in dark corridors and behind closed curtains to escape the sultan's notice. Their alert eyes watched his every move, their ears attuned to his every breath as he charged through the palace like a crazed bull, breaking everything in sight, swearing, making vows, calling out a name familiar to their ears, one that evoked a deep fear. The old among the servants recalled seeing the man behind the name when he had still been alive, others only after he had died and become a ghost, the most fearsome ghost. Some still remembered how he had enslaved them and burned their villages to the ground. The Spotted Hyena. The sultan was calling out to him, his voice utterly devastated: "Come right this minute from wherever you are – the sky, the earth, the sea!"

Mutei approached the sultan cautiously.

"Mutei, you wicked slave. Where are you?" the sultan shouted.

"I'm here, Your Blessed Majesty."

"Go and prepare the carriage for me. I'm going to town. I'll do away with all the negroes myself, and I'll get that stupid, depraved whore back. I told her she should live with me in this palace, and she refused. This is what happens when you disobey your parents. Get out of my face, you stupid eunuch. Don't just stand there like an idiot."

Mutei went to prepare the carriage as soon as he received the order. The sultan didn't notice him leaving, nor the wide, gloating smiles that flickered in the dark. He didn't hear the muffled laughs of the delicate young men and beautiful women behind the doors left ajar.

THE DAUGHTER'S PALACE

The recently blessed princess had no children, and she didn't know whether her husband did, with his many concubines in every corner of the world. His trade often took him travelling, and like many of his peers he wasn't faithful during those trips, given his divine right to marry multiple women and to have sexual relations with anyone in his keep. A child of his could be enslaved and working in a farm beyond the sea, or on this very island. Men who sired children by slaves didn't claim them as legitimate offspring; they were considered slaves too and sold in the market along with coconuts and cloves.

Her husband was the descendant of a wealthy family that dominated the trade of clove, ginger, and coconut. In his desire to marry her, the princess saw a desire to rule. She was the sultan's only daughter and the sultan himself was an only child. She knew full well that he only wanted to bear children to inherit the sultanate. If her father were to die tomorrow, her husband would become the sultan and she would become one of his many wives who crowded the harem. His desire for the throne was his weakness; he wanted nothing more than to rule these islands that endlessly abounded in gold and slaves. It was for this reason that he readily agreed to her request for fidelity. She made it clear to him that if he broke his promise, she would tell her father about his wives and his debauchery with slaves, and she would leave him.

I'll kill you if you don't do as I say.

He didn't believe her, of course. It was the same hollow threat he had heard from countless jealous women. He knew how to placate her with gifts.

Her words tended to slip through his mind without making an impact. But that day she surprised him.

"Today you must choose between me and all of your whores."

He fell silent. They were drinking coffee after a day in the countryside, visiting a holy spring to make an offering for a wish that had come true: a major, very favourable deal. They deposited two Maria Theresa thalers into the pond. It was meant to be a delightful, carefree time for them to share together, but instead of celebrating his success, she began asking questions he couldn't answer.

"You're the one I love," he said with a faint smile. "You're my eternal wife. The one I will walk into heaven with on Judgement Day."

"It's me or your wanton women. You choose. I'm talking about here and now. What happens in the afterlife is unknowable. At this moment, it doesn't concern me."

After a brief pause, he replied solemnly, "I choose you."

She approached him and he felt the warmth of her breath. "Only me," she said.

"Only you." His throat and tongue turned dry.

"Well then, you'll sell all your concubines and slaves, the ones here and in Oman, and in the harem in your father's palace. Yes, I know about them all, so I hope you will be honest with me. You'll hand over the money you earn for them, and I'll buy jewellery and garments befitting a sultana. What do you say, sultan?"

She doesn't understand the way men think, and why would she? She doesn't know any men. But I know how women think. They're deficient in mind and faith, captive to their desires. That's what the Bible says anyway, and why hell is full of women. Women and stones. They're jealous, frivolous, loose-tongued creatures who only care about nonsense. What if I've had sex with maids and the like? What of it? A man like me who fearlessly rides the waves, hunts animals and slaves, and faces death every day? To be hers alone? Has God not granted me the right to marry two, three, even four, as well as any woman in my possession? Should I break my word to her, I wouldn't be at fault. There is no shame in deceiving a woman for the sake of pleasing God. Only ruin and destruction await me if I displease him. Better to be a liar and a perjurer.

She's my wife, and my favourite one at that. She's sharp, kind, and virtuous. And one day she'll make me the sultan. No other woman can do that for me. The others

I simply lie with. I have no responsibility and feel no emotion towards them. They're mine; I bought them with my money, and I have every right to them.

Sooner or later, the ghoul will die. No one lives forever. I'll be patient. The opportunity to rule will vanish if I don't take a leap. A man ought to listen to his wife's words and then dispose of them in the deep bosom of the sea.

"I'd do anything for you."

"I'll kill you if you don't do as I say," she said with a smile he couldn't decipher. "That's a promise I'm making in front of the holy spring."

Then she burst out laughing. He laughed too. And they drank fine wine acquired from Italy, served in clay cups. It was brown and tasted a little like honey. He noted for the first time that it resembled blood, fresh blood from a slaughtered animal.

As the sun began to set, they made their way back to the palace on the backs of donkeys. The princess was drunk, and Sondus walked closely behind her to keep her upright. He had to be available at a moment's notice.

Of all the features in the princess's palace, the most beautiful was the enormous reception hall. The high ceiling, held up with luxurious marble columns, lent the hall more grandeur, helped by a mirror that covered the wall facing the front. It was, in fact, seven rectangular mirrors brought from England expressly for this purpose. There were ornate seats, some made of African bamboo, and many valuable antiques from the many countries visited by her husband, others which were wedding gifts from her father, and a few she'd inherited from her mother, whose death had been untimely. Her mother had been enchanted with hunting and had been the only woman to accompany men on hunting trips. She was also the first woman to hunt an elephant with a rifle. Perhaps it was sadness that had killed her when she discovered that it was the last elephant on the island.

The princess lived in the north wing. From the spacious balcony on the second floor she would look over the waves, the ships, the skies. She loved the sight of vessels fading into the sea, gradually, as if falling into an abyss, and the sight of them appearing from nowhere, approaching the coast. The sound of crashing waves charmed her, and the howl of storms, and the call of seagulls soaring freely. Her husband didn't care for such things. He was a practical man of the first degree. All his energy he poured into trade; his only joy was winning lucrative deals. He loved adventure and seafaring. His world was over there, at sea; his demeanour was sometimes closer to a sailor's than a wealthy merchant. But ultimately, life for him centred on wealth and power. Therein lay all his sorrow, his joy. Nothing else mattered.

In a fertile valley a short distance from the palace was the clove and coconut farm they owned. This too had been a gift from the sultan, who owned all the land on the island, which he sold and leased as he pleased. The management of the farm was delegated to Mariamo, an Ethiopian slave known for his tyrannical treatment of enslaved workers.

None managed to escape; he had eyes everywhere, and, if they tried, he devised forms of punishment no human could withstand. And yet he forgave them acts of theft, big and small, and allowed himself to steal too, as long as it didn't affect the annual income from the farm; or rather, as long as it went undetected by his masters. What Mariamo absolutely did not tolerate were certain acts of depravity, which for him included smoking tobacco mixed with Indian cannabis. He believed it brought bad luck. He once hung a boy by his feet from a tree and left him there overnight, only to discover later that nothing was left except his legs; the hyenas had devoured him. Had bad fortune befallen the boy, or had he brought it on himself? Mariamo didn't hesitate to submit anyone who broke this rule to the same fate.

You may steal tobacco from the master's farm, or cannabis from mine, but you cannot mix them in your pipe, or misfortune will befall you before it does me.

Mariamo had every intention of fleeing as soon as he collected enough silver and gold. He wanted to go to Ethiopia and leave behind this oppressive island of bad omens. He wanted to invest the money he stole, which he felt he had every right to. But when the chance arose during the British invasion of Angola in 1890, he didn't return to Ethiopia. He took his fortune across the ocean to Tanganyika, where he bought a farm and lived out the rest of his days with a young woman he loved, and who loved him despite his age and gave birth to two of his children. He died in Dar es Salaam, and the dream of returning home was buried with him.

Despite the hatred Mariamo harboured for Sondus, he admired his silence, his ability to stay out of others' way. Mariamo envied him for the privilege of living in the palace and always being by the princess's side; for his beautiful clothes and his softness; for the gold earrings that dangled from his ears.

I'm happy with my life at the farm, but this happiness demands everything I have, the small and big things I steal; the creativity it requires to hide that; my unrelenting work, day and night; my patience with the ungrateful, grumbling, narrow-minded lowlifes – nothing pleases them! They're always waiting for a chance to steal or to run away. That eunuch loafer, on the other hand, has everything he desires without any effort worth mentioning, with his silence. With nothing but his silence.

THE GOOD SLAVE

The forces of Omani slaver and elephant hunter Thu'ban bin Kuleib, the Spotted Hyena, surrounded the villagers like a ring around a finger and captured them all. They terrorised the villagers and their animals, birds and trees with weapons the villagers had heard of but had not laid eyes on. They heard that these machines would kill in a flash and permanently disfigure those who survive. They heard that their horrible sound was enough to make one lose one's senses or go mad.

Although the Spotted Hyena had died a few years earlier from malaria, he never abandoned his army. His ghost led them in battles. He was there, plain for his soldiers and victims to behold. While he couldn't himself fire a gun or slaughter or rape, he stood at the forefront of his troops; his cries could be heard in the midst of battle, and he achieved his greatest triumphs. He was said to have rebelled against the angels in the netherworld, that his evil spirit had broken free and returned to Unguja. What could the villagers do but surrender?

Everything of value was taken by the slave hunters, so long as it could be stored away, sold, or subjugated. They left behind the sick and elderly. All that remained was a wreckage of empty houses, the cries of the dying, the eagles patiently waiting to feast upon their bodies.

The leader of that village, who became Mutei, and his youngest son, who became Sondus, were the only villagers to remain on the island. The rest were shipped to Europe and America, where there was a pressing need for free labour in the constructions of roads and ports, in factories and farms, in medical research and the development of drugs, and in homes.

It freed those of us with the gift of intellect to devote ourselves to the advancement of humanity, to live the life we deserve. What do negroes do, after all, besides wasting away in no man's land, in the bushes and jungles of Africa, practising devious black magic, eating, dancing, and fornicating?

Sondus could not comprehend the position he found himself in. He didn't understand what it meant to lose one's freedom. Nor why he had been castrated at the same time. What did the two have to do with one another? Why did they shackle him and whip him for the slightest error?

When the slave trainer brought Mutei to see Sondus, Mutei said, "Son, you're a slave. You don't belong to me, you belong to the master, and he is like a god. Everything belongs to him. You must obey and serve him. My little Nano, you must be wondering why this happened, and the answer is that the master is more powerful than you. It's the same reason the fox eats the rabbit, and the lion eats the fox. The master is even more powerful. He kills the rabbit, the fox, and the lion, and kills us whenever he pleases. He owns the gun that shoots. Do you understand? With God's blessing, the powerful will always feed on the weak."

Sondus wanted to ask his father why they had castrated them both, but he couldn't utter any words and the questions continued to burn in his mind, filling him with hatred and fury. He wanted to ask: *Why doesn't God kill the master? Isn't God more powerful? What does "with God's blessing" mean?* But he simply nodded to show his father that he would do as he was told.

"Good. You will accompany the princess from now on, and you must serve her well. You must be honest and loyal and never attempt to escape – that's the only way they'll release you from these chains. If you try to run away, they won't hesitate to cut your arms and legs off, and then they'll cut off your head. Do you understand?"

Sondus felt the ghost of his missing part. Warm tears sprung to his eyes and fell onto his swollen cheeks before falling onto the chains and vanishing slowly.

"Everything we have lost is in God's keep," his father told him, with a strange calmness, on the way out.

Sondus was nine years old and the princess was twelve when he became her servant. She was thin with a wheat complexion and dark, shoulder-length hair. She talked and played endlessly. Since her mother had died during childbirth, she lived with her father and an old servant from India called Maya. The princess's mother might have caught a glimpse of the princess during her final moments, between hallucinations of slain animals, but the princess could conjure no image of her mother.

The princess had always wondered about Sondus's inability to speak, but they nonetheless were on good terms. He was a good listener and did everything asked of him. He made her toys from wood. She fed him all sorts of sweets and fruit, and when she started receiving lessons in Islam, fiqh, and mathematics, Sondus was allowed to sit nearby and listen. He memorised everything he heard, even though it was in Arabic, a language he didn't speak and neither did the princess. He couldn't fathom that there could be another God beside the God he knew, or that there were prophets beside the spiritual teachers his father had taken him to so that he and other children his age could be taught. He decided that this was the masters' religion, told in their language, and the Prophet was one of them. Nevertheless, Sondus was lured by the peculiar, melodic way the teacher read the Quran. Whenever the princess felt the sporadic urge to pray, she would have Sondus pray with her, and he stood behind her praying earnestly to his own God, the God of the jungle that had abandoned him and handed him to the slave hunters. He asked many questions in silence and they, of course, went unanswered.

There are more pressing matters than the questions I ask.

Sondus's relationship with the princess's body began only after Maya's death, six years after Sondus joined the service of the palace. Up until then, Maya had taken care of the princess's every need: she fed her, bathed her, brushed her hair, massaged and perfumed her body, washed and ironed her clothes, hummed old Indian lullabies to put her to bed. The princess didn't give any thought to replacing Maya, who was like a mother to her, with one of the many concubines and slaves who worked for her father. Why bother? Why couldn't Sondus help her bathe? It had continued to gnaw at the princess that the sultan hadn't granted the old woman her dying wish of being cremated with the sandalwood that she had spent years gathering, and for her ashes to be scattered in Kosala, or in the Indian Ocean. Instead, she was hastily buried in the slave and non-Muslim cemetery, on a rocky hillside a short distance from the coast. Her father wasn't present for the burial, which was carried out by a group of slaves and attended only by an old Indian man who had known Maya for a long time. What the princess did not know was that three days later, in the same manner as the character in the novel *Guardian of the Cemeteries* and Jesus in the Bible before them, the old woman had stood up. She hovered in the sky awhile, like an angel casting a loving eye over the island, then she visited her favourite corners of the palace, stopping to pat the princess on the head and to kiss her cheeks, two lingering kisses, before being whisked away by soft, warm winds toward her village, Manaskriti. There, her weary soul merged with Brahma, and she found eternal peace.

Upon hearing the princess's call, Sondus came running and found her naked in the bathroom, which contained a large bath that could fit up to five plump, languid adult bodies, such as those belonging to masters. The bath was made of colourful marble, at the centre of which was a seat built into the ground. There was a water boiler on the left wall, a large aluminium bowl sitting on a coal burner used both for heating and to illuminate the room. The bowl was painted blue and showed drawings of large, colourful birds in the style of classical Indian painting. Perhaps Maya had painted it herself or had had it painted. The bath had been built during her service, before the princess was born. Sondus's eyes widened as they took in the princess's naked body and he was about to turn around, but she said, "Come and wash my back. Take your clothes off and jump in. Don't be shy."

It was not out of the ordinary for Sondus to see the princess nude, and he had certainly seen his fair share of naked bodies over the course of his life. What had shocked him was the position she contorted into, sitting on the small marble seat with her legs spread wide. Maya had probably seen her in every posture imaginable, but she was an old woman who treated her like a daughter. Sondus, on the other hand, was assumed to feel no sexual desire, and if any such thoughts occurred to him at all, it was assumed he would not act upon them. He was castrated for the purpose of remaining close to the princess. Her father rarely came to see her at the palace, satisfied as he was with the knowledge that guards surrounded the palace and a eunuch kept her company. Neither male nor female, eunuchs are like a castrated ox, which made them good companions for young women.

The princess herself had been cut at the age of seven, like all the daughters of masters. Not that she perceived it as a disadvantage. Her mother, and perhaps her grandmothers before, had been cut, and if the princess gave birth to a girl, she would be too. They say these were the Prophet's instructions. The princess didn't know much about Islam, but she felt compelled to adhere to its teachings, trusting the omniscience of God. She believed it had been necessary to be rid of this devilish body part that would tempt her and lead her astray.

"It's okay."

Sondus felt out of sorts but tried to compose himself. It was not the sexual nature of the scene that took him aback, but the disregard the princess was showing him. A woman shouldn't reveal herself to a man who wasn't her husband.

But you're no longer in the village. You're the master's slave; you must do as you're told.

Her body was soft and clean. It shimmered like gold. For the first time, Sondus noticed that her breasts were lighter than the rest of her body.

"Get in the water. It won't kill you."

She sat on her knees and instructed him to pick up the scented soap and rub it on her body. To his eyes, she didn't need to be cleaned, and he worried that his large, uncared-for palms would make her dirty. At her incessant prodding, he started rubbing her body more diligently – her scalp, under her armpits, between her fingers and toes. He poured lukewarm water on her face. He rubbed soap on her buttocks and noted the smallness of her body compared with the women he knew. He washed her chest, as firm as a papaya but tender, which made him smile, and his smile made her laugh. They splashed around in the water.

A new bond formed between them, though on the surface Sondus behaved as any servant would. But soon a change came over him. He no longer saw his role as imposed upon him by the fact of his enslavement; his tasks began to feel like acts of love for the princess – the princess's body, to be more precise.

He brought her food.

He washed her hands before and after she ate.

He made her fresh mango juice, which he prepared himself with a wooden spoon.

He sat close to her and anticipated her next request.

He accompanied her everywhere – the market, the beach, the port.

He saddled the donkey and helped her mount it.

He listened to her hum Uhuru's songs.

He ran her bath and prepared her menstrual rags.

Together they caught little birds, fireflies, and hail during the rainy season.

He build her toys from bamboo and the wild fruits of the teak tree.

Her fat, despicable father occasionally visited with Sondus's father, who seemed to be getting heavier. Sondus listened to the sultan and the princess talk about everyday matters. Her father erupted: "If only I'd had a son! A girl is nothing but a scandal waiting to happen."

Her body communicated with him in an unspoken language only he understood.

She laughed.

Her eyes filled with tears.

She glided past Sondus, naked, like a cloud.

He fanned her to keep the insects and the suffocating air away.

He rubbed her back, her neck, and caressed her breasts. He observed them growing, their colour changing over time.

He watched her sleep and observed her breath quicken and her eyelashes flutter while she dreamt.

Her body seemed at times docile; at times it seemed to flit around like a hummingbird; occasionally it looked deadly.

Sondus loved her body in the morning. With the first rays of sunlight, her body bloomed, a petal at a time. Her blood stirred awake; the fine veins gently caressed her limbs. He knew the movement of every muscle, slow at first then gathering energy. He liked the slight redness in her eyes that faded as the day went on. She shielded herself with her hand from the light pouring in through the northern window and yawned. He hurried to draw the curtains. She lifted her torso and reclined on her back. He glanced at her breasts, recalling all the shapes and shades they had adopted over the years. The skin surrounding them changed from pink to white to blue to brown to pink again to purple, to colours he couldn't name. He couldn't be sure whether they were real or imaginary. Colours still to come.

He helped his mistress untwist the sheets from her body, which bent like a creek running over rocks on a beach. Sondus helped her up, and she softly placed her feet on a floral Persian rug. Whenever she stood up, the smell of her body was potent. It didn't matter whether or not it was a pleasant smell. To Sondus, it was exquisite. It breathed life into him. It jolted him awake, like morning coffee or the call of the rooster, like liquor intoxicating the body. It carried him home, where he picked wild fruit and chased monkeys and squirrels. He glided like a falcon, feeling a deep connection to the skies, his birthright and eternal home. He breathed in every trace of her scent. His lungs expanded like two sacks of sacred buffalo skin. For a moment he stood still, in contemplation, feeling the ghost of his missing part, the ghost that lived in his mind.

He would pray.

He would pray for the black African God asleep in a remote cave.

For the lush trees that swayed in the wind.

For the scent of mangoes, clove, and ginger.

For birds chirping.

For the dewy green grass.

For the ocean that ushered in the breeze, the fish, and also the slave hunters.

For the slave hunters and clove and ivory merchants who had brought the princess to the island.

For the Arab God who blessed the princess.

For her father.

For the iron chains.

For his forlorn and submissive father.

He would pray quietly while his thoughts grew louder.

She extended her right hand, and he caught it eagerly. Her hand contained the softness and delicacy of all that was new.

For breakfast the princess liked to eat goat's cheese, goat's milk and slices of wild goat meat, prepared by a team of mistresses, who then presented her with fruit and lemon tea. Before she ate, she always gave thanks to God, as Maya had once taught her.

"The God you know is the God we know. Hindus, Muslims, Taoists, Sikhs, Christians, Jews, and pagans – we have different ways of praying, but it's the same God that graces us with his love. God doesn't need our prayers or our gratitude. He exists independently of his creations. His existence is the beginning of everything, and our existence is secondary. We have no connection to God, nor are we worthy of it. God transcends connection and the need to connect. Such concepts are human, temporal. Our need for God is our source of comfort. We are God, but God is not us," she remembered the Indian servant saying.

"I don't understand," said the princess.

"Maybe not, but you've kept something of what I said."

"How can that be?"

"Because of prayer."

The princess prayed and thanked God that she hadn't been born a servant or a slave, and she hadn't been born to jungle dwellers who worshipped idols, and who were vulnerable to being snatched away to work without pay or thanks or mercy. She thanked God for keeping her in his grace by making her the sole heir to the great Sultan Suleiman bin Salim, descendant of King Solomon. She prayed to God and studied the Quran even though she didn't understand it. She even had Sondus convert to Islam. He never took the shahada because he couldn't speak, but they did pray together, and she was certain he was memorising the Quran along with her. Who cares whether he uttered it aloud? God heard the unspoken.

She thanked God that she had been born on this paradise. Uhuru's song sprung to mind and the princess's heart was seized with dread. She stopped praying. "Sondus," she called out. "Samahani, Sondus. Forgive me," she said, her voice dropping to a whisper.

Sondus stood, bewildered. He didn't understand why she was seeking his forgiveness.

Does a fox ask the rabbit's forgiveness as it gleefully devours its flesh?

He didn't say anything – he couldn't – so he pretended not to understand. Then a question occurred to him: *Which one of us owns the other?* Although the answer ought to have been clear, he couldn't come up with it. For a long time, he'd been feeling that the body she occupied belonged to him. It was not his body, it was a body he owned. He was its master, as the slave hunters would say. It was a body he had bought and enslaved using his power; the power his father had always talked about. As long as she dwelt in that body, she was his. He called out inside himself: *I'm your master. You are my slave.* He burst out laughing.

"What's funny?" she said, taken by surprise.

He fell silent, looking at her in astonishment. She returned the same look and tried to read his face.

"Have you lost your mind?"

Sondus hid his face, maybe out of embarrassment or out of fear that she'd know what he was thinking. They might cut his tongue off – it sat there doing nothing anyway – and drill a hole in his head to remove these sorry ideas, one by one, and burn them to the ground.

Roughly five years prior, on a sweltering summer day, the sultan had visited his daughter unannounced. It was a month after her twentieth birthday. He brought what he considered to be good news.

"A kind and honourable man from a respected family has asked for your hand in marriage" he announced after coffee.

"Who said I wanted to get married?"

"Marriage is a family matter," the sultan shot back, surprised by the quickness of her rejection. "I came here to share the good news. If you don't marry, our family will fall into oblivion. I'm an only child and so are you, and we must create an heir in order to survive."

"Now is not the time."

He laughed and stood up to leave. "You may think whatever you like, but you will be married. The truth is that I'm getting older and weaker. God has mercifully given me an offspring and I need to have an heir to the throne before I die. My grandfather worked hard to build this sultanate. I can't let it slip away because of you. So, tell me whether you'd like to meet the groom before the wedding."

A month or so later, the small island celebrated the princess's wedding. It was an extravagant celebration, and everyone participated by singing, dancing, and offering gifts – which was obligatory. Such occasions revealed who was faithful to the crown and who was not.

The enslaved children raced each other on donkeys and camels. Fishermen on small sailing boats played pirates and merchants. The older slaves played the circle game, which was only enjoyable to the spectators. The slaves ran around a large circle, and the winner was the one who remained standing despite the dizziness, sometimes nausea, and complete fatigue. Some fell dead because of their weak hearts. The sight of them running around like drunks never failed to raise howls of laughter from the masters.

In every corner of the island, the palace's band played. The slaves, some still chained, were forced to sing and dance on the streets and on plantations and in front of magnificent palaces. Uhuru sang her tamer songs about love and the ocean, but she didn't dance. At night, the streets and alleys were lit up. There were old fireworks brought from China especially for the occasion. Early the next morning, the newlyweds boarded a ship to Muscat and from there to Cairo for their honeymoon.

TUG OF WAR

I don't know what goes on in that silent creature's mind. Strange, sinister things, I'm sure. He makes me so uneasy. If it weren't for her, I would have sold him to the first slave hunter I came across and had him banished to a cotton plantation or coal mine in America.

*

He talks endlessly, like a grinding stone, and he won't stop coughing. He doesn't even bother to turn away when I'm near him. He coughs in my face when I bring his tray of food and when I bend down to clear his table. It hope it's tuberculosis or one of the many diseases the seamen bring from God knows where. I wish the ocean would swallow him whole and rid us of him. I hate seeing him parading around, naked as the day he was born. If it weren't for the princess I would have run away, but I won't now. I can't leave her behind; she's mine. It's him who needs to leave. I know she doesn't want him, that lice-ridden donkey. The perfumes he douses himself in will do nothing to hide that. He soils her with his body. He's not a master, he's just a slimy seaman.

*

You're desperate to become the sultan; I know that. That's why you married me. Yes, I've discovered my body through you, but that's not everything. Your body is filthy, your mouth smells foul because of the tobacco you chew day and night, because of the alcohol you drink, and because of the emptiness of your soul. Maya always said a pure soul shines through the body and a foul one reeks of decomposed rats. All these women who sleep with you have no other choice. Or do you think they can't help themselves when they catch a whiff of you or see you in your ragged clothes? Maybe they find the smell of putrid tobacco irresistible. I know you're lying about having cut ties with them. But you're not the only one who knows how to lie.

*

When the master wasn't home, Sondus was full of life. He and the princess's body reconnected – it alone made him feel like a complete human, with a body and a soul. Sondus did the same things whether or not the master was present: he bathed her, cleaned her nails, washed her back, touched her tenderly in an outwardly innocent and childlike manner, the truth of which was clear to her but not to Sondus. What Sondus missed was the smell of her body in the morning.

When the master was there, he sullied her with his stench. It turned Sondus's stomach. He would rather have stood all day in the slaves' outhouse than be in an enclosed room with the two of them.

"Why don't we have one of the maids from your father's palace take Sondus's place, and have him join the guards? His silence makes me uncomfortable."

"His silence is the most beautiful thing about him. He can keep a secret, and he can't use magic. How in the world is Sondus bothering you?"

"He scares me," the merchant said, feigning drunkenness. "I don't know what he's thinking. I'm afraid it's the calm before the storm. The sea taught me that the sound of waves can be deciphered. But if the sea falls silent, you ought to be very afraid."

"Let him be. He is just a little dim, nothing out of the ordinary. He doesn't mean any harm. I'm sure of it. Think of him as an inanimate object, neither male nor female, or an ox. I use him like a tool. I need him to serve me."

She knew her despicable husband couldn't be trusted in the presence of any woman, and this was another benefit of keeping Sondus close. Her husband lied and lied and lied. Even if he had sold his concubines, he was still the same lecherous man.

The princess wanted to keep Sondus for another, more complicated reason that she couldn't articulate.

*

If I had to choose between him and them, I would choose Sondus, without a doubt.

*

If I had to choose between her and freedom, I would choose her.

*

Life waits for no one. There are no second chances. Either you live it the way it should be lived, or you waste it forever.

*

He drank Cuban rum with a group of travelling merchants who filled the upper deck of the old ship and caused a racket. He wasn't the richest among the merchants, but he was the most influential given his recent marriage to the princess. For this reason, the merchants respected him and penniless women showered him with affection. The women were skilful in seducing men with their soft, coquettish voices, their sultry glances. Those who could sing, dance, or tell stories were at an advantage. As for what lay between their legs, as the seamen said, it was a gift from God granted to all women equally.

Despite the good company and fine rum, Sondus kept appearing in the merchant's mind, silently standing in front of him, studying him closely with his large eyes, vanishing and re-emerging at a whim.

When I become sultan, the first thing I'll do is send him on a journey of no return. And I'll send her to a harem.

Vintage wine from Britain was brought out. Once the merchants drank it, and everything else in sight, they turned their attention to drugs imported from Oman. The women they clasped in their arms didn't partake unless coerced. The men were always looking for the perfect sexual encounter, and the women knew that. During these encounters, however, the women's minds wandered to the children they had left behind in towns and villages on the mainland.

The men ate to their hearts' content, a feast of seafood and salted meat. They were like walking corpses, ravaged by alcohol, travel, the sea, and money. They began to doze off, and the women were spared. The merchant dreamt, as he always did, of Sondus and the princess. He watched them in his cabin on the ship while he sat on his bed cooking a large tuna on low heat, smoke filling the room. He jolted awake, body shivering, heart pounding in his chest as he realised the tuna was in fact him. He uttered a few unintelligible words and embraced the unfortunate woman near him. Gradually he fell back asleep, but this time his snoring was much louder than usual.

Pulling herself free, the woman rose to her feet. "This is not normal!" she shouted.

THE SORCERER

Sondus dashed through the jungle on the back of a donkey to find the sorcerer known as the Old Man. He set off early in the morning, while the temperature was still mild, and by the time the sun reached the middle of the sky, he had arrived at the small farm where the sorcerer lived. The Old Man wasn't old. He had a thick black beard and a head full of hair. He wore a large blue linen gown and no headdress. Upon arriving, he greeted the Old Man with a nod and handed him a letter written in Swahili. The Old Man offered him some water.

"We know you. We've been trying to reach you, but now God has sent you to us. I know you don't talk, so listen carefully to what I'm about to tell you and commit it to memory. They will come to the village in the dark of night, upon the tenth sighting of the crescent. They're your kin, Africans from the mainland. They're on a special mission, and they want to help you, so join them. What we want is to free our home from the invaders who enslaved us, killed our animals, and stole our land. It won't happen overnight – it needs careful planning. I'm a slave on my ancestors' land, Nano, working for nothing. You and your father are the sultan's slaves. We break our backs to fill the invader's pockets. Do you understand? All we need from you is to leave the armoury in the princess's palace unlocked. As you know, the sultan has filled it with weapons. Leave the guards to us. We know how to deal with them."

Sondus nodded. A tear fell onto his cheek. The sorcerer went on talking, then sat to jot down a letter for the princess. He handed it over.

"I'll send someone to deal with her request. She's a kind girl, but she lives in the seed of evil with her wicked husband and her father, who is even worse, a coward and a murderer."

The sorcerer continued.

"It's different on the island now. The Europeans aren't buying and selling slaves any more. They only stopped once they had used us to get everything they wanted. And it looks like they're no longer supporting the sultan, but he can still benefit them, which means they will do what they always do – they'll make him the ruler and pocket all the profits."

He paused for breath before pushing on in a low voice.

"We have to be ready. Do you understand, Nano? I'm talking about a revolution. I'm a man of the revolution, not just a sorcerer." The Old Man's throat caught.

It was all very perplexing to Sondus. He'd never heard this kind of talk. It had never occurred to him that he could one day be free. No one ever cursed the sultan or even referred to him as anything other than the Blessed Sultan, at least to his face. How could they possibly face the sultan's forces? How would they bypass the garrisons stationed in every corner of the palace to monitor the slaves, to keep them in line and stop them from running away?

With the rooster's morning call and before the tender sound of the adhan called Muslims to prayer, an old woman sent by the Old Man arrived at the palace. The princess was still asleep when the guards came in to inform Sondus of the old woman's arrival, but on these occasions, when such distinguished guests were sent, it was permitted to wake her. Sorcerers were revered across the island. People believed in their power to bring about good and to cause harm, so they sought their favour.

The woman was called into an external guest room. She declined the chair Sondus offered and sat on the carpet. A sheer veil covered her face and made her look Omani. She placed several potions on the ground and requested a large basin. Sondus brought one over. She then requested a jug of ocean water. Sondus instructed a guard to fetch some from behind the palace. She poured all the water into the basin, and it morphed into a diorama of the ocean. She added a salt-like substance as she uttered unintelligible words and performed something like a dance while remaining seated.

After a long pause, the old woman said, "Your husband is here now, in this basin."

"Where?" asked the princess, peering in.

"He's at sea. You can't see him, but I can. Children would be able to see him too. He is aboard an immense ship heading eastwards, maybe to India or even further."

"What is he doing?" asked the princess. "Who is he with? Any women?"

"Yes, there are women of all shades."

"Is *he* with a woman?"

"Blessed Princess, men are wicked. The ocean breeze stirs their desire, and the jinn that rides the waves on the winds of storms adds fuel to the fire. It's the jinn the Arab seamen brought with them hundreds of years ago."

The princess was deep in thought. "I want him to die," she said. "I want him to come back a lifeless corpse."

Sondus shuddered, seized by fear and a vague pleasure. He hated the master and wanted to be rid of him, and he had heard with his own ears that the master wanted to get rid of him, but Sondus never imagined it would end so violently.

"I know. The sorcerer told me," said the old woman.

"But I don't want to kill him with my own hands. I couldn't bear that."

"The sorcerer knows that. That's why he sent me."

"Let him die far away from here."

"The sorcerer will take care of it."

"How much does he want?" asked the princess, her body trembling.

"Two rifles and some ammunition."

"Two rifles? What will he do with two rifles?"

The old woman answered calmly. "The sorcerer can't kill him with his own hands – unless you instruct otherwise, of course. When it comes to black magic, one must do as one is told and not ask questions."

"Will he go to find him in the ocean?"

"The ocean will bring him to the sorcerer."

This was music to the princess's ears; she liked her answer and admired her composure and the beautiful fluent Swahili she spoke. The princess had always delighted in the varieties of Swahili.

Let the sorcerer kill him wherever he is, using any means necessary, but far away from me.

"Sondus, take her down to my father's armoury and let her choose two rifles, and give her two large bags of ammunition."

They wrapped everything in a large piece of leather to hide it from the guards. The old woman rode away on a donkey. No one knew where to. It wasn't only Sondus who soon realised the old woman was none other than the sorcerer himself; the princess did too. Sorcerers were known to take different forms.

A group of distraught seamen rushed in to deliver the news that the princess's husband had died, along with a few other merchants, possibly as a result of drinking contaminated alcohol. They said the body had been taken to his father's house. The princess sighed deeply, an involuntary liquid escaped her, and she fell and remained unconscious for two days.

THE REBELS

Ten months after her husband's death, the princess was still without a spouse, and her father was growing more fearful about his lineage. Despite his visibly strong appearance, he was like a giant tree with a rotten core. There were multiple reasons for his state: the British, the French, some alarming activities by black dissidents, and, of course, his daughter.

The French had begun frequenting the island more regularly as tourists and diplomatic delegations, spies, and scientists. This displeased the British, who descended upon the island in January 1883 with a new treaty in hand. It was purportedly about ending slavery. In reality, it granted the British full control over Unguja, its land and seas, making them the de facto rulers and turning the sultan into a mere puppet. They wanted to take away his heaven on earth. Ending slavery would mean taking away the mainstay of the sultanate's economy and putting the sultanate at risk of collapse.

A young British consul appeared at Paradises Palace one day, and asked the sultan for a palace to lease to house members of the British consulate and visiting officials, knowing well that there were no vacant palaces. What he meant was one of the occupied palaces.

"We'll see to it," the sultan said. "Allow us some time."

The sultan thought immediately of the princess's palace. She could finally come to live with him. He'd dedicate an entire wing to her and build her a modern bathroom and a kitchen with the latest appliances. What else could she want?

It's better if she's closer to me. I'm getting older and I need a daughter to care for me, instead of women I have no ties with except in the bedroom. And one day I'll no longer be able to do that.

His daughter had grown accustomed to his fleeting visits that had an ulterior motive. After offering him coffee as she always did, she asked, "Tell me, Father. What do you want? You seem preoccupied."

He talked about old age and the trials of life, about the precarious position the sultanate found itself in, about the British, the French, the Germans, and the Belgians, about dangerous dissidents. He told her he feared for her, and for himself being far away from her. He told her he wanted her near, that she must leave the palace and live with him at Paradises.

"Is this why you've come here?"

He didn't respond.

"I'll never leave this palace. It's my eternal home."

He talked about the dwindling revenues due to tight British surveillance targeting any ships leaving Unguja to cross the Indian Ocean. He told her about the spies monitoring the ports, and the inevitable economic collapse once the negroes earned their freedom. At that point, production would cease because immigrants were unaccustomed to working. They were effective overseers so long as they held rifles and whips, and had an abundance of chains, but no one among the soldiers from Sudan and the Swahili coast and the servants and non-Arabs knew how to read, write, or do basic arithmetic.

"We made a grave mistake by not preparing for a day when we would have to work with our own hands. It's now clear that slavery will come to an end. You know what this means. We'll try to bargain with the British and French, and show them what they stand to gain. They may sympathise, but it won't be forever. Things can change very quickly. We must endear ourselves to the British, my girl. We must win them over. That way they'll crush any possibility of a revolution by the negroes. They'll protect us from the ambitions of the French and Germans. The British consul once said to me that as long as we stand with them, we'll always rule this land. They'll make sure of it. They've done the same in many regions that have gained independence from them, given power to the traditional, historical rulers. Like you and me. In short, I want to lease your palace to the British consul."

"Are you afraid of the British, Father?"

"I'm not afraid of them," the sultan said, his voice rising slightly. "I'm thinking about the fate of the sultanate. The

British are straightforward. They know what they want and what their strengths are. I, too, am straightforward. I know what I want and what my weaknesses are. My weakness *is* my strength."

The princess's gaze turned to the ocean. Through the window she saw a ship cleaving the water towards the harbour, flying the flag of Great Britain, which danced gracefully in the breeze.

"I know that, but I'm not leaving the palace, not even for the queen herself. Give them Paradises Palace or the King's Palace, or any of the palaces on this island. Everything here belongs to you. Isn't that what you always say?"

"That was before the British were here! Before their frigates found these islands!" the sultan whispered. He looked at her intently and added, "You must do what is best for the island. Think about the common good."

"Ours or Britain's?" she scoffed.

The sultan stood up slowly.

Mutei hurried over.

"Get ready to move to your wing in Paradises Palace within a month. I must take care of this."

No one could have predicted how this conflict between the princess and her father would end. After all, the British consul was certain he would get the palace – specifically, the princess's palace. Its location and closeness to the harbour made it possible for small ships to arrive and leave in secret. The palace was remote from the muck and noise of the town. Above all, the consulate's security official had recommended it. He knew everything there was to know about everything.

Ultimately, what put a swift end to the debate was the unforeseen and vicious attack by the African rebels. They raided two armouries, including the one at the Blessed Princess's palace, and kidnapped her. It was on this day that Sondus spoke for the first time in more than ten years. When he found himself standing before the rebels, he cried, "Wait! I'm coming with you, and I'm taking the princess with me."

During the attack, Sondus witnessed a scene that would have caused him to burst out laughing were it not for the sheer terror he felt. The rebels arrived on a dark night, the first night of the lunar month. The soldiers were taken by surprise and didn't put up much of a fight; they were intoxicated, their mouths filled with khat, cannabis smoke circling overhead, and were utterly astounded to find themselves imprisoned and their weapons confiscated. They were gagged and tied up with ropes. However, a surprise awaited the rebels when they entered the palace. Upon stepping into the vast, majestic reception hall, they saw a mighty group of soldiers with fierce expressions, sparks flying from their eyes. The rebels were stunned to see that these soldiers looked just like them.

The rebels vanished at once, stumbling through the gate, avoiding a clash that would have certainly ended in defeat. Sondus caught up with them, calling for them to wait. He explained to them that they were merely looking at their own reflections in a magical surface that the invaders had brought over from across the seas - the big mirror that imitated whatever stood in front of it.

They came back and raided the armoury.

"POWERFUL WORDS UTTERED BY A WEAK MAN"

When the sultan reached the centre of town, it was teeming with people. The atmosphere was one of panic over the previous night's news. No one had realised anything was afoot until that morning, the sultan later learned. That was when officers had opened fire at non-existing targets to cover up their blunder.

The rebels' attack took less than half an hour. They walked away with many rifles and much ammunition, and they kidnapped the princess, before disappearing into the dark like bats. No one chased after them – not the soldiers, nor the townspeople. The only ones who even saw them were the guards and officers whom the dissidents captured, tied up, and gagged.

So precisely had the attack been executed that the sultan could only blame the British wishing to frighten him into handing over the island. The British, on their part, pointed the finger at the Germans, who controlled Congo and parts of Tanganyika. To the British, the rebels might have crossed back and forth from Tanganyika through the narrow gulf, supported by a European power attempting to destabilise the region, such as France, which had had its eye on the sultanate and had been aching for the opportunity to get its hands on it.

Two slaps from the sultan's blessed palms landed on the chief officer's delicate face and made its hennaed beard quiver. The chief officer was ordered to evacuate with his family back to Oman with nothing to his name, as penniless as he had been when he left. A British general who had held a security post in India was appointed in his stead upon a swift and strong letter of recommendation from the British consul.

The sultan offered an insincere apology to Great Britain for the accusations he had made, which he directed instead towards "terrorists" whom he promised to make pay dearly.

For the first time in years, the sultan walked around town on his own two feet, inspecting the official armoury on the western part of town, a short distance away from the princess's palace, which he had not yet visited because he didn't want to reveal the secret of the weapons he kept there. Later that evening, he made a separate visit to the princess's palace. As expected, not a single gun or bag of ammunition was left behind. The sultan ordered for his daughter's belongings to be moved to his palace, and for preparations to be made for the British consul to lodge there. The consul welcomed the idea and thanked the sultan.

The sultan made his way to the mosque accompanied by dignitaries, merchants, and travellers, his personal servants and hefty black guards headed by Mutei. The masters entered the mosque, leaving the servants outside. Eunuchs weren't allowed to enter the mosque or participate in rituals that require purity; the reason given was that they couldn't control their urine and therefore could never be truly clean. Other servants, however, were allowed to pray in the final rows. The sultan performed the noon prayer, then gathered his immediate circle.

"We are surrounded from all sides by the enemy – Europeans and European-supported Africans from the mainland. They claim to defend human rights, but they seem to have no issues with trampling on our legitimate rights. The enemy surrounds us. There are frigates on the water and spies in our midst. They gnaw at us like insects, even though we share the same skin. I'm talking, of course, about the white-skinned enemy with the black heart. But there's an enemy far more dangerous, which is ignorance. It has spread among us. Tell me, can your children read and write? Have they learned a trade? The enemy has coerced us into signing treaties that only serve their interests. They want to consume us like fire consumes tinder. Look at what happened to the clove trees and to the land! Where has the rain gone? They destroy our land and provoke God's anger. Now is the time to ask the question: Who are we? What do we want? Do we want to remain here or leave forever? This land was built with the sweat of our grandfathers' brows.

They rescued its savage, ignorant natives from the darkness of the caves and brought them to the light of civilisation and Islam. And now we've lost it all. Our army – who is our army? Are any of your sons in the army? Our officers, who are they? The doctors are Indians and Westerners. The farm workers are servants, Swahilis and Sudanese. I could go on and on. Now I must be honest and admit I had a part in this. Like the rest of you, I live a life of comfort. I don't even know how to mend a pair of shoes. Write this down, Sheikh. Yes, in Swahili. 'All Arabs capable of taking arms must join training camps immediately. Anyone in possession of weapons must hand them in to the chief officer and receive proof for having done so.' The day has come for you to protect yourselves. As you can see, my daughter was snatched away while the guards stood by and did nothing. Would they have done that if she were of their flesh and blood? No. Every farm owner must work on his farm for at least one day a week. He must learn from the workers. The day has come when he can no longer rely on slaves. Everyone must learn how to make a living.

"I fear it's already too late. You were once masters, but the day has come for you to bow down to a master. You were once strong enough to make the Portuguese kneel before you. Now it's you who must kneel before the British. I fear we will become Africa's Andalusia. Its leaders doomed it to oblivion with their insanity and despondency. They thought the sword and whip alone were enough to protect them and their sultans.

"Write this down. 'Leaving the island is prohibited for all except the deposed chief officer and his family. They must leave it with nothing on their backs, barefoot, penniless. Those who want to leave may do so without any of their possessions, slaves and male offspring. Those who were born here must die here defending their home.'

"'Every citizen must donate five Maria Theresa thalers to the war effort. Every tribe's sheikh, every governor, every chieftain must apply these policies as of today. They're to report to the sultan at Friday prayer next week. The head captain must prevent any citizens who are breaking the rules from leaving the island on ships.' You've reaped the fruit of this island. You've tasted its honey. Now you must try the sting of a bee."

When this speech later landed in the hands of a British spy, sealed by the sultan's stamp, he laughed and said, "Maneno makali alisema mtu dhaifu." *Powerful words uttered by a weak man.*

THE STATE GOVERNS ITSELF

"I'll get her back. My only child. The future of my great grandfathers' sultanate. The Spotted Hyena is after them. He'll catch them and we'll lynch them on the mango trees in the market. We'll let the hungry raptors feed on their bodies. No, we'll tear them apart ourselves. We'll sever their arms and legs, gouge out their eyes, and crucify them. We'll charge them with acts of terror, then we'll burn their bodies stiff," promised the sultan.

"Spotted Hyena, shrewd warrior, hunter of humans, beasts, and jinn, where are you? They couldn't have done this without black magic, and maybe the British. I don't know where in the world my own jinn was, and why it didn't intervene. Even my jinn has deserted me, betrayed me!"

He muttered incoherently while Nurah rubbed his back. Though she was his favourite, he often forgot her name, as he forgot the names of others. The women didn't bat an eye when he called them Fatuma Jama, the only one whose name he never forgot. In moments of heightened passion, he used her pet name, Mamo Fato. That's what he sometimes called the young Englishman in his harem.

"There are two things that obey the law of inertia and don't require real governance: my ninety-nine women and my sultanate. As long as everyone does their part, the state governs itself. Should one fail to do so, they'll only harm themselves. The life of a master is a simple life. Masters manage their farm or trade through their slaves. And they manage their women and offspring. The women are there for the master's joy and for producing children as well as for working and earning money. Yes, the slaves do everything on behalf of the master, who only acts as supervisor. If the master gets angry, he takes it upon himself to punish the errant slave, child or woman. Every woman knows when it's her night, and gets prepared for it. She takes her time preparing a good meal, chicken or goat meat. She takes a long bath, shaves her hair, and puts on perfume. Some women love to entertain the master with folk tales. They know better than to ruin his mood by making demands. They know there's a time and place for that – the grand Eids of al-Adha and al-Fitr."

Life had always been simple. But once the Europeans had arrived on the island, the sultan was faced with tough decisions that required tact. He had to navigate the conflicting interests of all parties in order to protect his own. He had to put an end to the slave trade, but without giving up the slaves. He had to give full control to the British, but also to protect the sovereignty of his land. He had to build a modern state in order to maintain his sultan-style rule. And now a new problem emerged: the sudden upheavals of the native Africans. What did they want? Who stood behind them? The trickiest problem of all was the kidnapping of his daughter. Should he rely on a ghost to bring her back? Where the hell *was* this ghost? Could he cross to the African mainland, where the negroes had taken his daughter, even though it was now in the hands of the vicious Germans?

The beautiful woman, his companion for more than ten years, rubbed sandalwood on his old, tired back. He was trying to recall her name when Mutei walked in to announce the unexpected arrival of the British consul.

"He's waiting in the reception room."

The sultan muttered "I seek refuge in God from the accursed Satan" as he walked to his closet. As Mutei helped him dress, he recited the Throne Verse repeatedly. He was certain the consul didn't come bearing good news; he never did, that omen of disaster.

It had been three months since the palace had been given over to the consul and his guests. As luck would have it, two of the so-called guests had died after drinking contaminated alcohol they'd found hidden in the palace.

"What does this have to do with me? They didn't get it from me. Why were they rummaging through the palace to begin with? In fact, according to the terms of the lease, the rooms on the lower level were off limits. One might even say they were spies who made a mistake and suffered the consequences."

"That's not quite right, Your Highness. One of your men, perhaps your spies, poisoned the alcohol. The departed had every intention of paying for what they consumed. But let's say they did steal it. Is it Your Highness's position that death is the appropriate penalty? One can't help but wonder why you keep contaminated alcohol hidden in the palace you lease to the British consul and his guests. All the palace contents had been inventoried. Here is a copy of the inventory. It doesn't include poison or guns. Her Majesty is expecting an explanation from you."

"What unrelenting curse is this that has befallen me? Frankly, I don't know what to say."

"That's an acceptable enough answer. All you need to do is pay compensation for the grieving families. I must warn you, this will cost you."

"But I didn't kill them."

"It is your legal responsibility nonetheless. You are the ruler. 'All of you are shepherds and each of you is responsible for his flock.' Isn't that what your book says?"

The sultan was sure that wasn't in the Quran, but he didn't want to delve further into the subject. Instead he said, "All that lies within the premises of the consulate is under the consul's responsibility. This is mutually agreed upon and signed. We have a copy of the lease."

The consul smiled. "Let's take it to the British court then. I just want to remind you that those found guilty of premeditated murder face the death penalty, while in the case of manslaughter an appropriate compensation shall be paid to the family of the deceased." Before excusing himself, he asked, "What is the penalty for stealing alcohol here?"

"Alcohol is prohibited here," replied the sultan without thinking.

"This is what I find most puzzling. If alcohol is prohibited, why is it kept in a palace leased by the British consul? Why is it imported to begin with? What do you do with it? Even the most seasoned British judges would be confounded by this case. It makes sense to encounter a vial of contaminated alcohol in a lab, but what is it doing in the palace belonging to a devout Muslim sultan? This would simply bewilder the European mind, which respects logic. Should you wish to settle the matter, we are ready. But it's up to you, of course, if you'd prefer to wait for the ruling."

What do these Europeans want from us? The island is ours. We built and developed it, and we now rule over it. The land and the people belong to us. We never asked the Europeans or anyone else for anything. We did everything on our own. Our grandfathers sailed across seas and sacrificed their lives for the island. We planted clove trees we brought with us. We reclaimed this wasteland. We rounded up wretched negroes from the jungles and had them cultivate the land. We spread the Word of God. Then the Europeans appear out of thin air to meddle in our affairs. Would they ever allow us to meddle in theirs? Britain goes on colonising most of the world. It sold millions of slaves. It murdered, exiled, and displaced. So why can't we do as we wish in our own country? We didn't deal in slaves, but we kept the ones who were here, already in our possession. We have the legal right to them. We are God-fearing in our treatment of the slaves. We've never treated them the way Europeans and Americans did. We abide by God's word and the Prophet's Sunnah. Yes, there are exceptions. We're only humans, after all. We make mistakes.

"We have repeatedly urged you to accept Britain's protection over the island, but you keep resorting to elusive tactics. You have to pay generous compensation to the families of the two deceased. This will be the equivalent of two palaces: the princess's palace and Paradises Palace. You can keep the King's Palace and the Palace of Wonders. This deal will also cost you two thirds of your farming land, fields, and forests. You will now have to accept at gunpoint what was offered to you on a golden plate. We read your speech as a unilateral declaration of war. What else would be the purpose of militarising citizens? What war are you preparing them for? Against whom? We're closely following your secret interactions with the French, who outnumber the trees on your island. But these games will get you nowhere. Our advice to you is to accept British protection over the islands. If you don't, you will have to face the English frigates. You know the language of their artillery very well," said the consul. "I wish you a good day. Our apologies for disrupting your afternoon."

The sultan resorted to prayer. He sought God after the ghost of the Spotted Hyena deserted him. The jinn that carried out his tasks in moments of need no longer answered his call. A sorcerer had once said to him, "Black magic doesn't work on white people. That requires white magic, and the demon responsible for white magic doesn't live in Africa."

He spent his nights reciting the Quran, asking God to save him from the British and their schemes, from the negroes and their rancour, from the French and their malice, the Germans and their brutality. He remained in this state, fasting all the while, for an entire month, until once again the consul interrupted him one afternoon and announced that his property had been transferred to the families of the victims. He informed the sultan that he must vacate the palaces as soon as possible. That's when the sultan lost hope in prayer. He blamed no one but himself. From now on, he decided, he would try to get closer to the British. He would obey them and heed their call. The only thing he wouldn't do was accept their total protection of the island.

The sultan signed over two of his palaces and two thirds of his land. The British freed his concubines and gave each one some money out of the sultan's wealth to help them resume their lives. He was allowed to retain only two. As a gesture of goodwill, the British authorities also allowed the young Englishman to remain, and he agreed, perhaps with the encouragement of the consul.

"Will the British help me get back my daughter now I have submitted to them?" the sultan asked.

"This would be possible had the rebels not taken her to lands under German protection," the British consul replied. "All the information we have tells us they crossed to the mainland. We know they're armed, and that the princess and her servant are with them. The officers didn't find a trace of her. The kidnappers disappeared like the wind. That's what we learned from General David, the new chief of police, who did everything in his power."

"If I were stronger, I would have assembled an army and crossed to the mainland and come back with my daughter. I would have made those criminals pay. Unfortunately, one can't count on the support of others in a moment of weakness. If I were strong, everyone else would be at my service: people, demons, even God," the sultan said out loud to himself.

It didn't occur to the sultan, distressed over the loss of his daughter, to think of the thousands of people he had separated from their families and sold in markets like cattle. It simply didn't strike him as anything out of the ordinary. Were it not for the frigates of those ex-slavers, he wouldn't have discontinued the slave trade; wouldn't have closed the big markets spread across the island, run by professional slave traders. He was now certain that the main reason behind the collapse of his rule and the loss of his huge fortune was that he had been forced to sign the slave trade abolishment treaty even though he didn't fully abide by its terms.

"Is history showing me its sour face now? Has the balance of power been disturbed? Surely life on this earth is unpredictable. Nothing lasts forever, not even the most noble values. The British banned the slave trade, but we ended up becoming their slaves. We used to scorn negroes for their colour and docility, and now we're even worse in the eyes of the British. We, being Muslim, thought we were superior to idolaters, but the British now see us as a bunch of non-believers in Christ. Instead of us preaching Islam, they're the ones preaching Christianity to us. I dread to think that one day we'll be ruled by those we ruled for centuries. The balance has been disturbed. It has to be the work of some jinn. Wake up, people. Snap out of this daze you're in. Damn you all!"

Mutei was listening to his master think aloud from his bed on a scorching summer morning. Humidity was high and the sun's rays were flooding the suite the sultan had moved to after his palace had been taken over by the British. The sultan couldn't sleep a wink. He hallucinated all day, calling for his daughter, screaming at ghosts that crowded his room, ghosts of demons, es and Omanis, elephants, trees, Englishmen. What scared him most was the ghost of the young British consul and his constant, unnerving smile. The ghost of Mamo Fato gave him some solace.

"Mamo Fato...Where's the princess? Where's my daughter, for God's sake?" He burst into maniacal laughter at seeing two ghosts he knew very well, who were engaged in a vicious fight over a clove tree. He felt sorrow at seeing the ghost of a young African woman whom the Spotted Hyena had arrested and sold to him but who had bled to death after a sexual encounter with the sultan. She had left behind a child who had disappeared one day. It was said that his grandfather had sneaked into the city disguised as a roaming sorcerer and taken him back to the village. Perhaps one of the slavers in the palace had sold him. Or perhaps he had died.

The sultan suddenly yelled at Mutei: "Why haven't you brought the shit receptacle? Why are you standing like a statue? Get the hell out of my face!"

Mutei stood looking at him in a bemused and sarcastic way, then asked, "Where is my son?"

The sultan was stunned. For the first time in his life of more than a hundred years a slave was directing a question to him. "Your son? Who's your son?"

"Sondus!"

"Are you going to interrogate the sultan about your son, who kidnapped my daughter and ran away with the savage negroes to the mainland? Who knows what they're doing with her now? They might be roasting her flesh to eat her. You should be asking about the princess, your and your son's princess, you ungrateful bastard."

"He's my son," Mutei replied coldly.

"You don't have a son! You're my and my daughter's property."

"And you are a slave of the British," replied Mutei, shaking with rage.

The sultan slowly rose to his feet and struck Mutei in the face. "This is what I was afraid of. A slave less worthy than the dirt under my shoe is talking to his master and the master of his people since the day of Adam until Judgement Day." He beat Mutei ruthlessly, kicking him with his fat legs and hurling at him everything he could get hold of. It was as if he was crushing the British consul to pieces, or spitting on the British crown, or having sex with the cunning old queens of Europe, or urinating on an English frigate lurking in the ocean, waiting for the right time to attack him, or slaughtering his daughter's kidnappers with his pure gold dagger that he hadn't unsheathed since he had received it from a roving Indian goldsmith.

Upon hearing Mutei's screams, the guards rushed in. The sultan ordered them to take this mutinous slave to the underground prison and leave him there and throw his dead body to the dogs. Then, like a wounded wolf, he howled: "Wait a minute! I said wait! First whip him until his skin tears apart, and then piss on him!"

Two strong-bodied prisoners took him where dozens of prisoners had been kept and presumably beaten to death before being fed to hungry dogs. Those were the same prisoners Mutei had been taking personal care of for many years, feeding them from the leftovers of the royal dining table. The food was carried every day from Paradises Palace to the King's Palace, where they were kept. It was a single meal a day, but a luxury for prisoners who were sentenced to stay in the prison until they rotted.

The sultan never visited the prison himself. It was said he couldn't stand the sight of his own victims. The mouth that spelled out verdicts was different from the eyes that would watch the verdict being carried out. He didn't even know the prison's exact location. All he knew was that it was located somewhere in the basement of his palace, and that whoever was to be sent there would only come out of it as a rotten body to meet the dogs.

THE PRINCESS ON THE AFRICAN MAINLAND

Instead of sleeping, the princess sat gazing at the sea, listening to the waves and distant seagulls, and watching the lights on ships coming and going, becoming gradually dimmer before being swallowed by the horizon. She glanced at the lighthouses floating on the water, the waves playfully hiding them from sight. She contemplated the darkness of the night and the beautiful distant stars. She started to sing an African Arab melody:

> I love you, night.
> I love the stars hanging in the sky
>
> The light adorning your charming face.
> Your voice; the sound of wind, seagulls and waves.
>
> I love you, and I sing to the ocean wide
> I want to ask you—

Sondus interrupted, shouting, "I'm taking you with me!"

She couldn't believe the sound had come from him, the eternally silent Sondus. Had a jinn emerged from the sea in the shape of Sondus?

"Help me! A jinn!"

"It's me," Sondus said, his heart pounding. "I'm not a jinn. There's no time to explain now. The rebels are outside. Let's join them!"

"Who?"

Sondus took a few confident steps towards her and said, "You'll meet them soon." He didn't wait for her to make a decision or recover from the shock. Instead, he picked her up and rushed to her room. A scream didn't break from her lips; it was trapped inside as in a terrible nightmare. He placed her limp body on the bed. She stared vacantly, her mouth open like a fish dying on land. Sondus grabbed her most valued objects: a pair of shoes and a traditional flowy dress, and all the ornaments he could get his hands on.

They delved deep into the jungle, taking convoluted routes no one else knew, not even the sultan's soldiers. Sondus had estimated there were fifty rebels, but in fact there were a hundred. Not all of them took part in the attack; some waited at different points in the jungle and communicated with one another by making hooting sounds using antlers. Every group had its task, such as surveillance or providing backup in case the assault force was attacked. The assault force was stationed at the entry point to the city.

It wasn't the first attack carried out by the indigenous people. The first had occurred thirty years prior, headed by the great warrior Samba, though it had ultimately failed. He was pursued and defeated on the shores of the mainland by the sultan's army, Swahilis and Sudanese soldiers. Samba lost a great many fighters, but he managed to escape into the jungle. His goal hadn't been to capture weapons – it was to seek revenge on the sultan himself after he had cheated him in a deal involving hundreds of pounds of ivory and rare leather. No other major attack on the town ever took place after that, save for occasional skirmishes in the surrounding villages, especially during the drought, which prompted small hunger revolts. Those ended in the capture of all the rebels. They were fed until the glow returned to their skin, then they were sold in the slave markets.

The princess sat on her donkey, and Sondus sat behind to hold her up. The parade passed through narrow paths with dense trees, forming a straight line almost a kilometre long, the rebels singing war songs, carrying the rifles and bags of ammunition they had secured. They'd need the weapons in the long term, for purposes only the chiefs knew. They had done their job by finding the weapons; the rest of the plan was not any of their concern. As they made their way, the spirits of their ancestors protected them, covering their tracks from those who meant them harm. The rebels wore amulets around their necks, given to them by the sorcerer and chief of their village to protect them from snakes and scorpions and other deadly creatures. The African God who resides in a faraway cave had given them blessings and a number of rules to follow:

God only abandons those who abandon him.

Those whom God does not protect must ask themselves about the wrong they've committed.

Those who don't speak to God through their hearts, God will not look at with his eyes.

Those who knew the path of God and yet did not take it, and those who abandoned it after having walked it, and those who stole from their kin, and those who committed violence, and those who did not obey their chief – how would they navigate the darkness?

They felt no hunger or thirst, their bodies didn't tire, their spirits were high. They walked in silence, with their leader at the front. They didn't stop or look backwards – bad luck comes to those who expect it. Using boats that had been hidden in the thick coastal grass, they crossed to the mainland. They might have escaped the sultan's brutality, but there were the animals of the mainland to reckon with, animals that had been exterminated from the island through hunting over the course of many years. The island was small, but greed was vast, and no matter how enormous and ferocious, the animals were helpless in the face of guns. The massacres against animals continued until none were left in Unguja except for small numbers of monkeys, birds, and rabbits. Elephants were sold as ivory. Wildcats, giraffes, spotted hyenas, and ostriches were sold as luxurious leather. Peacocks were sold as feathers. Nothing was left of the elephant except its famous tale with the tiny fly, or of giraffes other than their image engraved in ancient caves.

The rebels loaded the donkey onto the boat. They didn't want to leave it behind since it belonged to a good breed brought over from Yemen.

At the suggestion of one of the rebels, water was splashed on the princess's face until she regained consciousness. "Where am I?" she asked in a hoarse voice.

"You're with me. You're okay," replied Sondus.

"You can speak!" she said, trying to make out his face in the dark.

"I can speak. It's a miracle."

"Where are you taking me?" She adjusted her dress.

"To a village on the mainland."

"Why are you taking me there?" she said, dismayed.

"I'm sick of living in a place where there are only two types of people: masters and slaves. I'm taking back my freedom. The time has come."

She drew in a deep breath. "Why are you taking *me*?"

Sondus hesitated, then said, "I want you with me. I don't know why." He couldn't tell her that she was his freedom, or rather that her body was. Had he known words like love and passion and lust, he could have expressed his feelings. Language didn't lend itself to him.

The rebels spoke a fluent Swahili, which combined several local languages, some English words, and many Arabic words picked from the mouths of seamen, merchants, masters, and slave hunters over the course of two thousand years. The princess knew no other languages. She read and wrote in the Arabic alphabet, which she had learned from her husband after insisting on being taught. He had thought that all books except the Holy Quran hid evil between the lines. He had thought such things corrupted women and made them insubordinate, giving the example of Sujah, a false prophet during Prophet Muhammad's time. Where would she have learned rhetoric were it not for the ancient books she read? The princess's father was to blame, according to her husband, because he allowed her to learn maths, astronomy, and even magic.

The princess had asked her husband, "Why aren't men corrupted by reading and writing?"

He had laughed. "Nothing corrupts men except the guile of women."

"I'll ask my father to send the young Omani faqih to our house to teach me," she replied. "Maybe he'll also show me the cunning prowess I possess."

Sondus had learned alongside the princess. The rebels, on the other hand, couldn't read or write. They had no need for it. They were fighters, farmers, and herders. Knowledge was transferred from one person's mouth to another's ear, and through daily practice. Morals and values were passed down from one generation to the next. At the age of ten, children were taken to educators, elders who drew symbols on the boys' bodies denoting their age. Every tribe had its own system of symbols, and children born in a particular year were marked with a distinct symbol. Children were taught good manners, self-defence, and the various means of livelihood available in their community. They were educated in essential disciplines such as fortune telling, tracing footsteps, the language of objects, and the language of nature such as seasons and the patterns of stars.

They came upon a narrow, sluggish river, where crocodiles were known to live. Thanks to the Portuguese, a small rope bridge had been built, which the nearby villages repaired every year in a traditional ceremony. Thanks to the morning light, Sondus was able to read the date of construction: 6 June 1660.

The Blessed Princess's eyes silently roamed as the surroundings came into clearer view. She saw trees she had never seen before, and wild animals unafraid of humans: gazelles, giraffes, crocodiles. What astounded her above all were the young, free negro men, none of whom tried to lay a hand on her as she had been anticipating. Her father and his peers, on the other hand, liked to declare that sex with prisoners of war was a legitimate right, that there was no shame in it. Her father's harem had fifty prisoners of war. Yet these young men didn't even gaze in her direction. By sunrise, they were on a vast expanse of land that started from the point where the sun came out and ended where it sank.

As the rebels approached the village, their voices rung out with songs, chants, and old incantations. They'd accomplished their forebears' and chiefs' dreams. Here they were. They had come back victorious.

The leader gathered the rebels in a circle and said, "We're almost there. But there's one problem – they're going to ask us about the woman. I think Sondus should be the one to explain. She's his responsibility, not ours."

Everyone except Sondus and the princess understood that trouble awaited.

ON LOVE AND FREEDOM

The princess was born on 5 October 1855 on Unguja, or Zanj Barb, the Negro Coast. Her mother, who departed too soon on the day of the princess's birth, was the sultan's only legitimate wife. The princess was the sultan's only heir. They say the sultan's obsession with sex was driven by a desperate desire to have a male heir who would preserve his lineage. He was adamant that his heir had to be male, while the princess was adamant about becoming the sultana, as many women before her had been.

"What about the Sultana of Mohéli? Djoumbé Fatima!" she once cried during a heated debate with her father.

"She's the reason I won't allow you to be my successor. Do you know how many times she's been married? She's an intelligent, well-regarded woman, but men don't see anything except her round arse."

Resisting laughter, the princess said, "Why do men behave this way, Father?"

"God made them this way. He does as he pleases."

"Then this is an issue with men. It has nothing to do with the female sultan."

"If she's to rule over men, it's her problem too. Men will do everything in their power to get access to that luscious—"

"What about Queen Elizabeth? Queen Theresa?" she interrupted.

"Listen. White women are different. They don't have bodies worth lusting over. Probably because of the weather. It seems they use up every ounce of fat in their body to resist the cold. In a way, they're closer to men than women. This is how God willed it."

"You're an old man! You'll never have a son. What do you expect to happen to the sultanate?"

"I'll wait for you to have a son, and he'll inherit the throne," the sultan replied, his voice steady. "Besides, God may bless me with a child, as he blessed Prophet Zechariah in his later days."

The sultan continued to take new wives and a great many lovers, but Fatuma was the only one who bore him a child. She continued to occupy his mind. Not only did he constantly forget the names of the other women, he also couldn't recollect where he had got them from, not even the ones who came from renowned families and who had pursued him out of greed for power.

Once he remembered the name of a woman and asked the harem's keeper to fetch her and bring her to his bed, only to be told she had died more than twenty years prior. "No one told me," he said.

"You led the prayer at her funeral. She waits for you at Sidrat al-Muntaha, up in heaven, with the other honourable women who passed."

The princess wasn't willing to give up on becoming the sultana. She knew it was just a matter of time and that nothing would come of her father's efforts to beget a child. All he wanted was to have his back rubbed, to be told stories, and to hear gossip circulating among women about what went on in his sultanate and on the surrounding islands. Until her father passed away, she resolved to enjoy her life, resting assured that one day she would rule over all the arse-worshipping men on the island.

It was after the death of her husband that she began to incessantly feel the needs of the body. Not that she desired any man in particular; her desire was located within. Perhaps she feared their ulterior motives given her position in society. She wore traditional Arab dress everywhere she went, which completely covered her. It was unbecoming for her to be seen, unlike maidens and slaves who were brought from across the seas for the purpose of pleasure. She had found pleasure with her late husband. His sporadic presence had suited her, but she had felt a lack of security, and the knowledge that he had been unfaithful was disquieting. Nothing distinguished her from all the women scattered across the earth and on filthy ships, except being the sultan's only daughter, and that made her uneasy.

The truth was that her husband had taught her a great deal. The skills of his faceless lovers were transmitted to her – Kama Sutra from the Indian lovers; tongue play from the Europeans; saying the right thing at the right time, which he had learned in Alexandria and Cairo. He had jolted her body awake after a long period of dormancy. And now, years after his body had been laid to rest, her body still burned with a volatile desire.

If there was one benefit to having married her husband, it was that she had become uninhibited. She would sometimes talk to her less fortunate friends, whose husbands didn't travel, about what they were missing, to make them lament their fate and lament the fact that their husbands hadn't learned anything of value from the women they had cheated on them with. She shielded her pain at her husband's promiscuity by saying what anyone in her position would say: "My husband learned it from all the books he reads." But the women knew her husband; the entire town did. They heard from their husbands the stories he would tell when he was drunk, stories that invariably cast him as the hero. It was said he was the only man who had slept with a woman from every continent. It remains uncertain whether that was the case. What was true, however, was that he was the only man in the so-called islands who'd had a concubine from China.

A strange thought struck the princess about the person in her possession, Sondus. She began to ponder the question: what *is* a forbidden sexual act? She was told it meant being penetrated by a man. But Sondus wasn't a man. She liked that his sexual advances were limited to timidly touching her breasts. She knew these touches belied a restrained, silent desire. Why not go a little further with Sondus to satiate her hunger, to allow their mutual, subdued desires to find a new, deeper expression? He wasn't a man; she owned him, and she had heard the faqih say that the reason adultery was prohibited was to avoid mixing family lineages.

Like her father, she wasn't truly devout. Their people were influenced by the language and culture they encountered in Africa, which led to believing in a mix of sorcery and the ritualistic aspects of Islam: prayer, fasting, hajj; and the societal norms of men and women, which had less to do with Islam and more to do with Arab and Persian culture. Though she wasn't religious, she sought internal peace. This didn't occur to her when she asked the sorcerer to kill her husband, overcome as she was by an inner force that banished any sense of right and wrong. She thought of it as a wild, satanic jealousy that had taken hold of her momentarily. Her husband would have likely called it the guile of women.

The voice of Maya came back to her: *Don't overthink it. Don't sit idle and wait for life to be fair to you. You seek your own justice. Don't hesitate.*

As for Sondus, his encounters with the princess were delightful and full of surprises. For the first time, he felt that the ghost of his missing part wasn't a hallucination; and the princess's body was a real body: alive, warm, hiding strange sensations. Her smell brought him to life every morning.

"Yes, there. Bring your nose a little closer."

At first, he was hesitant. He was terrified of making a mistake that could end in beatings or land him in jail or perhaps dead. If he were to get caught touching the princess's breasts, he could say he was simply washing her body, and it might have been believable, but to be as close as he was to such an intimate part of her body, caressing it with his tongue – what could he do but obey her order?

"If I tell you to do something, you do it." She kissed him on his hands and head. She ran her long nails through his hair and under his arms. She licked the part where his sex should have been, not sensing the ghost. She whispered in his ear, "How does it feel?"

The princess saw the answer in his dilated eyes, in the tremor that ran through his body and into hers, and in his rapid breaths. She wanted Sondus to feel pleasure. But she also wanted to know that he truly desired her, for him to take the initiative rather than timidly responding to her gestures.

She wanted to find answers to a question that troubled her.

Do I treat him as my property or my lover? Is he following instructions or acting upon his desires?

For his part, Sondus discovered a state of rapture. An enigmatic shiver that radiated through his body. A moment of disappearance from the world. For the first time, he experienced freedom as something tangible, a matter of fact.

Is the pleasure I feel a pleasure of sex or of dominance? My body merges with hers and I lose track of where mine ends and hers begins.

Here was the same God that had thrown him onto the slave merchant's boat now putting him at the helm and sending a favourable wind to take him back to the coast of freedom. Villagers received him and the princess with songs, horns, and drums. He wished he could kiss them one by one. Here he was, back with his woman. He wasn't sure what exactly he was going to devote his time to. Perhaps he would simply join everyone else in cultivating the land.

The princess clutched his hand firmly. She wanted desperately to feel protected. Everything around her was strange and bewildering. The people she had always thought of as barbarian magicians and cannibals were dancing and singing before her, praising God for bringing back their sons safe and sound, carrying weapons with which, as the rebels recounted during the journey, would liberate their land from the slavers and colonisers.

THE INCOMPLETE SOUL

The village people watched in astonished silence as the young men arrived accompanied by a strange woman and a boy with gold rings dangling from his ears, dressed in a silk jilbab and a turban. The villagers waited patiently for answers, knowing they would eventually come. They tried not to rush such things, having lived by the Swahili proverb "Haraka haraka haina baraka."

"Seventy rifles and thirty bags of ammunition. A job well done! 'When the donkey gives birth it says, "Now I shall rest",'" began the village chief, addressing the crowd. "Sons, you were very few, but as the saying goes, 'Two people are sufficient to restrain an unyielding buffalo.' You were prudent, well prepared, disciplined, and courageous. 'Beat a drum too loudly and you may tear it apart.' Today we give thanks to God, first and foremost, and to the souls of our ancestors. We give thanks to the mothers for their prayers, the sorcerers for their protection, and the teachers for preparing you for a life of hard work, obedience, and knowledge-seeking.

We thank the leader Mwana wa Imbowa. The soul of our greatest ancestor dwells within his youthful body, where it will live longer than a baobab tree. Young men, we offer our thanks to you. One day you'll become the leaders of your land. 'A crow never gives up its nest for the black stork just because it's larger, darker, louder, its beak longer. The crow fights until the end.'"

He continued: "'If you stay upright, no one can climb on your back, and if you want the sun to shine on you, you must leave your hut.' We, here, want the sun to shine on us. The road before us is long, but the longer it is, the more it teaches you. You learn how to fight hunger, how to overcome fear. Finally, we give thanks to the fathers who brought you up. Now, come along. There are things we need to discuss at great length, and we must do so without haste."

The young men had their feet washed with warm salt water, their legs rubbed with oil and splinters teased out of them. They were fed wild venison and goat; water, fresh milk, and wine. They fell asleep before the sun set. The princess and Sondus were offered separate huts, made from straw and bamboo, in the chief's compound. The villagers wondered about the relationship between Sondus and the princess, but they didn't ask. It wasn't yet time, and it was improper to question a guest upon arrival. They were to rest and become acquainted with their surroundings first. The guests, on the other hand, were expected not to wait too long before introducing themselves. A delicate balance of silence and patience was always at play.

In her sleep, the princess drifted to the palace, the ocean, and her father. It was the closest she could get to her world. She saw a large group gathered for a funeral of a woman who had been found dead on the shore. The corpse continued to chatter until it was lowered into the ground. It was the custom in Unguja for funeral rites to be carried out by men. Once the body was buried, the men returned to their homes, but a flock of eagles circled above the grave. The corpse emerged from beneath the ground, rid itself of its shrouds, and lay down for the eagles to swoop down on it while it went on babbling without pause.

Sondus didn't dream. He slept little. He couldn't stop thinking about the day of his castration. When he had regained consciousness, he'd heard his father say, "Everything we lost is in God's keep. One day it will be returned to you." It was a story those who had suffered castration found comfort in, convincing themselves there was a remedy to their loss. No one knew where the story had originated. It could have been as old as the practice itself, more than two thousand years. It had likely sprung up during a period of horrific violence on the island and the mainland. Perhaps it had been invented by a slave hunter who sought to placate the slaves. It had made its way into indigenous culture and become a firmly held belief. It was thought that if a eunuch finds their way back home, they could retrieve their missing part from God's caves, and if they died in exile, their souls could return on their behalf. An incomplete body was considered an incomplete soul. The act of retrieval completed both the body and the soul, necessary for reincarnation in the next life. Sondus was absorbed in these thoughts about his missing part, about his freedom. To him, the two were inextricably linked. He wanted to be free, with a body and soul that were whole.

Getting up, Sondus put on his Omani buffalo-leather shoes and his jilbab. They weren't perfectly clean as he used to keep them, but he had nothing else to wear. Outside, it was warm and the villagers were still playing drums and dancing a short distance away. The sound moved him; he longed for his childhood in the village. He thought of his father, still enslaved, and he felt his throat catch. He stepped quietly towards the villagers, keeping his distance. The need to find the chief and to tell him everything was growing more intense, like a pain in his gut.

Sondus couldn't see the village chief among the singers and dancers, young men and women dressed in soft goatskin, their chests bare, dripping with sweat. His mind drifted to Uhuru, to the market, to the old Indian merchant sitting bowed over his merchandise, to the slave chained to a steel wedge – the dirty, black mass of flesh.

He asked a young man where the chief's hut was, and the man took Sondus to it. It was larger than the other huts, painted with lime and decorated with carvings of giraffes, monkeys, and masked warriors. Atop the hut was a large pair of buffalo horns. The door was made of solid wood and engraved with a pair of spears. When he was a child, he had seen them on the homes of chiefs and the equally mighty magicians, who were often the same person, as was the case here.

A towering baobab tree stood near the chief's hut. Sondus recalled people in his village gathering under its shade to hold assemblies. It served as a court, the place where the chief oversaw the village's affairs. Sondus inched closer to the holy tree, taking in its peculiar shape. There was a spiritual and historical explanation for the form of every tree. The baobab, for instance, was the keeper of secrets, history, and spirituality. Village elders knew every inch of it, and carved it with symbols of important events: catastrophes, celebrations, marriages, births, deaths of sultans. Even if it hadn't been dark, Sondus wouldn't have been able to decipher those symbols, since every village had its own.

Sondus reached the hut, knowing the chief would be awake, and not questioning whether it was the right time to pay him a visit. It was the chief's duty to keep his door open at all times, unless he was in bed with one of his wives, in which case he devoted his attention to her. Sondus greeted him from the door and was invited in. He removed his shoes and his jilbab as a gesture of respect, so as not to appear better dressed than the chief.

The room was lit by an oil lamp. The chief sat on a large wooden chair in front of a table with clay pots of food. Behind him were his bed and a few plants. The room smelled of humidity, cloves, and mango. Sondus noted the pot full of mango pits by the bed. A sizeable snake, locally known as the puff adder and considered holy for carrying God's wisdom, was sound asleep under a large water pitcher covered by a metal lid. It was said that if you stir evil, it will never leave you in peace. That's why the snake wasn't to be disturbed.

The chief gestured for him to sit down, and Sondus chose a chair far away from the snake.

"I came to talk to you about something personal," Sondus began.

The chief looked into the eunuch's eyes, trying to gauge what he was referring to. "Go on, son."

"I want to get back my manhood."

The village chief straightened up and sipped his soup. "As you know, it's in God's keep. It's an arduous journey to God's dwelling," he answered calmly. "Go and rest. We can discuss everything at the village assembly."

"I don't want the whole village to know."

"The assembly must have a say. This is the way things are done here. If you want to achieve your goal, you must accept that. There's no reason to feel ashamed."

Sondus wasn't convinced, but he stood up to leave.

"Are you Muslim or Christian?" asked the chief.

"I don't know," Sondus answered begrudgingly.

"Do you know your tribe?"

"No."

"Show me your back."

Sondus squatted for the chief to study the marks burned into his back at his coming-of-age ceremony.

"You're twenty-five years old. You belong to the Zimbozi tribe. There are none of them left, I'm afraid. Almost all were enslaved, and those who got away fled to Mombasa." The chief didn't tell Sondus that a curse had been placed on his people, and that he carried it too. It would follow him wherever he went.

Later, Sondus still couldn't sleep, not even after the drumming stopped. Soon the sounds of hyenas travelled from the depths of the jungles. He remembered his mother, who awoke numerous times during the night to check on the chickens, goats, and the donkey, and on the children in their beds, and to see whether her husband had returned from hunting. He thought about going to the princess's room. He missed her breath, her warm body, her soft skin. And he was eager to find out what she was thinking about, how she felt. He stood up and paced around in the darkness. He put on his jilbab, cold but soft to the touch and still carrying the Indian scent he used to wear, the princess's favourite. He lifted his arm and plucked a bloodsucking insect from his armpit. He examined it closely and it emitted a noxious odour in self-defence, so he threw it on the ground without crushing it.

The moon disappeared behind the horizon. Darkness descended, engulfing the place in silence interrupted only by the howls of hungry hyenas, the wailing of the wind, and the frightened barking of indoor dogs. Leaving his hut, Sondus noted light coming from different parts of the village, small fires that kept deadly animals at bay. The princess's hut was directly behind his. He knocked with trembling hands.

"Sondus?" she asked.

"Yes, it's me."

Her room was lit with an oil lamp slightly smaller than the one he had seen in the chief's hut. The heat of the afternoon lingered inside. Her bed was bare and she was wearing nothing but a piece of fabric around her waist. There was no place to sit except on the bed. The sound of the hyenas and the dogs had been keeping her up, and she'd hoped he would come to see her.

"Why didn't you come sooner?"

"I had to wait. I talked to the village chief."

"About what?" the princess asked anxiously. "Are they going to sell me?"

"No, of course not," Sondus replied, surprised by the question. "It wasn't about you. We talked about me."

"About you? Aren't you one of them?"

"No. It's not that."

"Will you tell me what you talked about or not?"

"I'll tell you."

They fell silent for a while – a short while to him and an eternity to her. He took a deep breath.

"We talked about me."

"*What* about you?"

She caressed his hair and he pushed her hand away.

"Tell me," she said, inching closer and trying to kiss him.

"About my body," he blurted out.

The princess briefly fell silent. "I'm sorry, Sondus. My people are monstrous. But I'm yours regardless. You satisfy me as you are. Don't I satisfy you?"

They fell into an anxious silence. She tearfully put her head on his lap, holding his fingers with both hands. She placed her lips on his abdomen and bit him lightly, then sprang up, pushed him onto the bed, and frantically kissed him. She undressed herself then Sondus, manoeuvring his obedient, soft, warm body as she pleased. He submitted to her. He wanted her to devour him.

His mind wandered between yielding to pleasure and the task before him. The latter had become an obsession. He wanted to do what other men could do to the princess – even her pathetic husband. The image of his erect penis, wet with her fluids, overwhelmed Sondus with jealousy and nausea. He couldn't forget it.

One day I'll reclaim my member from the God's caves. It will be large, long, and erect, and I will let the princess taste it.

The princess, meanwhile, was savouring the strong masculine body that surrendered to her completely, unlike her late husband, who had denied her the pleasure of being in control. He couldn't suppress his dominant nature. She loved that Sondus yielded to her so completely. It stirred in her a deeply buried masculinity; the desire to become the kind of man who ruled over his ancestors' land, fulfilling her father's dream of maintaining the dynasty. A man, like her father, who lusted over women with well-endowed hips. She wanted to be both a man and a woman. She sucked the part where his sex should have been and rubbed his testicles, which the ruthless butcher had inadvertently left intact, unlike his father, who'd had everything excised. Sondus noticed a pleasant feeling around the ghost of his missing part. Moments later, his body ejected a fluid the princess had long waited for. She caught it in her mouth, driven almost mad by pleasure.

They were woken early in the morning by a knock on the door. Someone peered in, letting in the bright sunlight. Sondus and the princess were in the small wooden bed, naked in each other's arms. One of the chief's wives entered carrying the typical breakfast of the region: tea, milk, and ugali. She didn't seem surprised to see them. Later they would discover that she had gone to his hut first and hadn't found him there, and that the entire village had learned that he'd sneaked into the princess's hut at night. The villagers had wondered what a eunuch was doing in the dark with a woman.

It's not any of my business. In any case, it'll come up at the assembly.

"Good morning," the chief's wife said.

Sondus and the princess sat up with a jolt, unable to see the woman clearly because of the sunlight. They dressed in a hurry. The princess rushed to relieve her of the tray, while the woman's eyes sneaked glances at Sondus, trying to see what was between his legs, to answer the question on everyone's minds.

"Enjoy. Do you like ugali?" the chief's wife asked them.

"Yes, we do. Thank you, Mother."

It was clear from her crown of grey hair and the shape of her body that she was getting on in years, yet her face bore an unmistakable youthfulness, a beauty she would likely carry to the grave. The princess envied her for that beauty that defied ageing. She knew wrinkles seldom marked the sun-bathed faces of African women, especially if their teeth were intact. Some tribes extracted a few young girls' and boys' teeth, believing it added to their beauty, but this often distorted their facial structure. The chief's wife had full, bright teeth. She wore the bone of an animal on one of her nostrils. She looked innocent but was by no means naive. She had in fact fought her way through life, had managed to bring up fourteen children, feed them, and fill their heads with folk tales. Storytelling was the natural channel to pass knowledge from one generation to the next. A storyteller was infinitely wise.

That was how the story about Sondus and the princess was passed from tongue to tongue. This didn't reflect badly on the older woman. To relay something that one had seen wasn't frowned upon, as long as one didn't embellish it a great deal. Her embellishment was a minor one. All she said was that they hadn't noticed her coming into the hut, so engrossed were they in what she called "fornication". She said she had stood at the door in stunned silence and almost dropped the tray and spilled the milk on the ground, which would have invited a curse.

I had stopped believing there was such a thing as castration. I ask for your protection, Great-Grandfather, though I shouldn't invoke your name in circumstances so unworthy of you.

"We made a big mistake. What will they say about us?" said the princess once she and Sondus were alone. "From what I saw in the eyes of this woman, it seems we've made a grave mistake, haven't we?"

"I don't know. I suppose we'll see."

"I'm worried sick. I don't want any of this food."

"We'll never experience anything worse than what I saw in Unguja with my own eyes. Don't be afraid. Let's wait and see."

"Take this food and go to your room. Wait, no. Don't leave me here alone. Stay, but sit over there. You were wrong to bring me here with you, and I was wrong for coming. I just didn't want to be separated from you. I suppose I also wanted to escape the tedium of my life. I wanted adventure! It seems my mother's spirit lives on inside me. But now I'm scared to death!"

To Sondus's surprise, the princess fell crying into his arms. She had always been strong and composed. Even when she had been a child, she'd never cried. Her demands were accompanied with fury. Sondus was familiar with her anxiety and fear, and he had seen her coldly plot the death of her husband, but he'd never seen her break down, not even on the day of the kidnapping or on the day she'd received news of her husband's death.

"What are you afraid of? Is it that they've seen us here together?"

"No," she said, her eyes fixed on Sondus's.

"What is it then?"

"The woman!"

"What about her?"

"The way she looked at me. So full of hatred. I don't think we should eat this food. It could be poisoned. I know what they're like. My father always told me. He was afraid of them. The older they get, the more wicked they become. Witches! All of them. Every single one of them."

Sondus grabbed a large piece of ugali, dipped it in milk and swallowed it. Then he gulped the milk. "If I die, you should probably avoid eating in this village," he said with a chuckle.

The princess wiped her face and squatted on the ground. She poured water from the jug and washed her hands, said "bismillah". She dipped a piece of ugali in milk and took a hesitant bite at first, then greedily devoured the rest. Her hunger overwhelmed her fears, as it always did.

"We'll be cursed together or poisoned together. If this doesn't kill us, one of these villagers will."

As they ate in silence, Sondus's mind wandered back to his task. One day he would be a man, an ordinary man.

After he finished eating, he washed the cups and plates and set them aside, then returned to sit with the princess. The door was left ajar, and he pushed it open, allowing passers-by to look in.

"I need the bathroom," said the princess, a nervous smile on her face.

His expressions revealed that he didn't know what to do. They walked out of the hut, self-conscious about their filthiness.

"Sondus, do you think the chief's wives have bathrooms?"

"They have bathrooms, but not like the ones in your palace. They do the job. Go and see. When you come back, I'll go, or I'll just go in the jungle."

Shortly afterwards, Sondus picked up a clay water jug and approached the dense thicket surrounding the village. After checking for snakes and scorpions, he squatted behind a bush, still feeling eyes following him. He watched the villagers from his hiding place. The majority had left in the early morning to hunt or to work on the farms; the merchants among them had taken off to nearby markets. The only ones left were the sick and elderly, women on the cusp of childbirth, or those who worked in the village. There were only a few who were wandering around, but none of them spotted him or came to check on his hut or the princess's. His mind drifted to his father.

The sultan will never spare him, even though he had nothing to do with me taking the princess away. I've never known anyone more ruthless.

He recalled the sultan's face on the day of castration, calling Sondus a coward while he screamed, begging for mercy.

Does Father still repeat what the Arab prophet said about runaway slaves?

The slave trainer, a rambling, violent creature, had been charged with converting slaves and teaching them what little he knew of Islam: a few sayings linked to the Prophet. He sowed fear in their hearts about what would befall them on Judgement Day if they tried to escape. But he wouldn't give them the luxury of having their punishment put on hold until that day. They had to be punished before their departure to the next life.

Thoughts whirled in Sondus's mind: the villagers, the sultan, his father, hell on Judgement Day, the bleating of the slave trainer, slaves being burned, slaves running away, children being castrated, people being stuffed onto ships and carried into the unknown, the bells of slave hunters ringing, sultans laughing, villages being terrorised by the armies of Tippu Tip, British and French spies posing as tourists; sorcerers, rebels, and the God of Africa guarding a cave.

He felt something slam into him, throwing him onto the ground, his face landing on the hard ground. He slowly rose to his feet, disoriented and full of panic. A large wild boar, the kind domesticated by the villagers, was snorting and devouring Sondus's faeces.

THE VILLAGE ASSEMBLY

"Why did you bring this Arab woman?"

The chief put the question to the young men at the assembly. The young men remained silent. They had to wait for the chief to finish talking, then they had to hear from the married men, who spoke in order of age. Unmarried men were rarely called upon to contribute on matters public or private.

"This generation has no respect for our people's values," declared a toothless elder. "In all my eighty years, I've never heard of a man taking a woman from her family without asking for her hand in marriage and without paying a dowry. This is not our way. It's the way of the godless hunters. The devil himself created the hunters to go against the Gods of Africa. Were you possessed by their jinn? What madness is this? I prayed I'd never live to see this day. The curse we all feared is here. The same curse that befell the Zimbozi and drove them to the coast of Mombasa. May God protect my grandchildren, and may we never find ourselves in Mombasa, where the end of the world undoubtedly begins."

A slightly younger man in fishing gear stood up.

"War is coming. I can smell it. That sultan has captured thousands of us and wiped out entire tribes. He'll stop at nothing now. It's not about the weapons and ammunition those courageous warriors took. These will hardly trigger a war, but kidnapping his only daughter surely will. Are we ready for war? Can we stand to fight the army of the sultan and Tippu Tip? And why should we fight and die in a meaningless war? This woman is not one of us, neither is this Zimbozi boy. Why should we die for them? Why should we lose everything for some clitless Ungujan girl?"

Stifled laughs left Sondus feeling stung. As a member of a cursed tribe, a former slave, a wretched hostage with a disfigured body and soul, he felt he was also the target of the insult.

My own people think I'm a piece of shit eunuch with a void in my soul, and the Muslims of Unguja think I'm a worthless runaway slave destined for hell.

Once all the married men had spoken, a few single men were permitted to address the assembly. The elderly women took their turn, followed by the village sorcerer, who was also the singer. Sondus was called back to answer two questions: "Why did you kidnap her?" and "What do you plan to do with her if you can't bear children?"

A warrior known as Mwana Wa Bitch, Son of a Bitch, who had been sitting quietly, stood up, offering a brief apology for speaking out of turn.

"Do you know how many people this girl's father

enslaved, how many women he raped, how many young men he shipped away? Do you know how many people wake up and toil every day, shackled, starving, feeding on the remnants left by the grandchildren of the invaders? We sow, harvest, fish, hunt, fetch honey, make butter, raise cattle, work our fingers to the bone, and get nothing in return. Never do we even taste the honey and butter we make. For the first time since the Portuguese, British, Germans, French, Arabs and many others have set foot on this land, we've captured one of theirs. So my question to you is this: why don't you allow us to treat them the way they treat us? No one's blood is worth more than another's. No one's soul is worth more than another's. No one deserves to be a master, and no one deserves to be a slave, yet in our land you'll only find masters and slaves. The masters appear from beyond the seas. And when we finally bring you someone whose father killed, enslaved, displaced, and sold our people, all you can do is prattle on about right and wrong, about some curse?"

The villagers shifted uneasily. The chief paced back and forth. "When you do what the devil does, you become him," he said. "Would you drain all the water from the river if a crocodile killed your father? Keeping a woman hostage will bring a curse upon us. It would do no good to enslave her. She's not responsible for her father's crimes. Why did you bring her and not her father? Did you think of the harm you'd be bringing to your people? No. You chose the easiest path. Rest assured, the day will come when you can take revenge. Sooner or later, it's bound to happen. The culprits will be made to pay. But now we must do everything in our power to protect ourselves. Take her back to her family. It's the only way."

Sondus asked for permission to speak. "I want to marry her," he said.

Hands flew to mouths; chests were quietly shaking.

"If I marry her, there won't be a curse," Sondus said defiantly.

"Will you pay her father a dowry? Will he give his blessings for his daughter to marry one of his slaves? One who can't bear children?" asked the chief.

"I'll get back my manhood from God! I'm free now. I don't care about her father's blessings. I only care about her. She's mine, and I'm her master. I was once her servant, but I served her because she belongs to me."

No longer could anyone contain their laughter; some could barely control their bodily functions. The chief hushed the crowd. He silently tugged his short, coarse beard, plucking and tossing aside strands of hair. The villagers waited eagerly. He silently deliberated the real possibility of an attack led by the ghost. What if the sultan were to receive the support of the British or the French? What would happen to the villagers, so utterly unprepared for battle? The chief was in the process of gathering arms, but the arms they had gathered would do nothing in the face of a foreign alliance. The chief kept these thoughts to himself. He took refuge in knowing that some curses could be overcome by seeking closeness with God and offering sacrifices, but then it struck him that nothing would ever satiate the rapacious, bloodthirsty invaders. "Bring the girl," he finally said, trying to rid himself of that last thought.

"I'll fetch her," said the wife sitting near him, and hurried away.

"I don't understand what you mean when you say she belongs to you, but at the end of the day, we humans are limited. What you ought to do is seek God. God's knowledge, unlike ours, has no bounds."

Before Sondus could respond, the chief came straight out with it: "When you say she belongs to you, are you referring to what happens in the bedroom? If so, I understand you, but how does someone like you do that?"

"As you said, humans may not understand, but God does," said Sondus, trying to choose his words carefully.

The chief's wife walked in with the princess, and two other women carrying infants. The chief invited the princess to sit. Her hair was unkempt. It draped over her shoulders and covered part of her face. Her lips were cracked, and her complexion had turned ashen. She forced a smile as she lowered her body onto the wooden chair and looked at the chief expectantly.

"You're here against your people's wishes, perhaps against your own. For that we ask your forgiveness. We'll see to it that you return to your home, safe and sound, and we hope our people will be spared."

The princess replied in fluent Swahili with an urban touch. As a Murabu – an Arab born in Unguja, as were her father, grandfather, and great-grandfather – Swahili was the only language she knew. Mangha, on the other hand, were those who had been born elsewhere and migrated to Unguja then learned Swahili. The princess and her ancestors were Arabs of the African variety. The Islam they observed was one influenced by African traditional beliefs and practices. What separated them from the Africans around them was their grip on power: political, social, and economic.

"I want to go home. I can't live here – the life I know is very different. And my father won't be able to live without me."

"We'll take you back when the moon darkens again. Until then, you must live as we do. You must prepare your own food, fetch water from the well, wash your clothes. One of my wives will keep you company. Delicious food abounds here: grasshoppers, kababu, sweets, filuza, boudin, and dried fish. As you know, we're a long way from the ocean, and to be honest, we're glad to be. Delicious fish come from the ocean, but so do hunters of humans and animals. The ocean is our curse. We live in fear of it and are content to live without its offerings, but our children, our animals, and our land we can't live without."

"I understand," the princess replied.

"And you must beware of the hyenas and large snakes that can swallow you whole. Do not go out alone at night."

"I have nothing to fear as long as Sondus is with me," she said, glancing at Sondus.

"You too can go back with her," said the chief, following her glance.

"I'm not going back. Not before I get back my manhood."

"I'll follow Sondus wherever he goes," she said, searching Sondus's eyes.

The villagers began to murmur. A triumphant smile spread across Sondus's face. He tried not to laugh.

"Didn't you say you wanted to go back to your family?" asked the chief.

"Sondus is my family too. He always has been. If he goes back with me, I'll guarantee that nothing happens to him. If he doesn't want to go back, I'll go wherever he goes."

The chief tugged on his beard again. He pulled out two hairs and tossed them away. He spat out remnants of mango that had been stuck between his old yellowing teeth. "Now I understand," he said with a sigh.

Where there is smoke, there is fire. Only God knows how a woman can love a eunuch, and how they can make love. I wouldn't have believed it had my wife not seen it with her own eyes. This will be the source of the curse. It may appear in the shape of Tippu Tip's mighty army, which may be advancing through the jungle at this very moment. There will be those who show them the way to us.

The chief dismissed the assembly but asked Sondus and the elders to stay behind. The princess was escorted by the chief's wife, who rushed back to her seat, not wanting to miss a single word. The chief continued.

"Son, go away and take this curse with you. Take the girl wherever you want. To her father, or to Mombasa. It's a big city full of wanderers. You'll be among countless seamen, Arabs, Europeans, slaves, merchants, Indians. No one will notice you. You may even find one of your relatives. Mombasa was created by the jinn the Arabs brought with them. The Arabs went to the mainland and left the jinn behind roaming the seas, awaiting their return. So it followed them to the mainland and built them palaces. Take her and go. And be aware that Sultan Suleiman bin Salim will not give up his only daughter, heir to his sultanate. This girl who can barely wipe her own arse – *she* will become the queen of Unguja. French, British, Arab men will want to marry her. I fear that in the end you'll end up hanging from a tree, my son. This girl is bad luck. A curse is bound to follow, and our poor people don't deserve it. Do you understand me?"

"Yes," replied Sondus, "but I need one thing from you. I need you to show me the way to God."

"There are many ways to God. Not too far from this village, in fact, there's a well that leads to one of those paths. You can take the wooden ladder down into the well. But you should know that you might pay with your life. You'll encounter all kinds of deadly obstacles. You'll see things you can't even conceive of. But if you live to see the end, you'll restore your body and soul."

"Explain it to me. How exactly will I restore my body?" Sondus asked ruefully.

The chief placed a piece of tobacco in his mouth, along with a piece of natron. He returned a terse smile to Sondus's bright one, using his tongue to manoeuvre the tobacco.

"Shawiri ya Mawjudu," he said. After a while, he added, "Come and see me on Saturday morning, before sunrise but after the rooster stops calling and everyone leaves for work. After the ants and mosquitoes go to sleep and the owls fall silent, and the bats hang upside down on the mango tree. Bring with you a twig from a Mkunazi tree and one from a Yobishka tree, and some coconut water."

THE ROAD TO GOD

Early on Saturday morning, just before sunrise, as the birds began to tweet, Sondus got out of bed. With the rooster still crowing, he splashed his face with cold water to wash away the tiredness and the nightmares. Walking out of his hut, he saw the villagers leaving in droves, farmers to plantations, hunters to the jungle. Sondus stood by a mango tree and glanced at the bats hanging off its branches. He no longer heard the crow, only the hens and chicks clucking, and was certain the tiniest insects had fallen asleep, and the owls had gone quiet, so he walked towards the jungle. Not too far from where the wild boar had attacked him, he found an enormous Mkunazi tree, embraced by thorny branches. It had no fruit and its leaves were scattered on the ground, announcing the end of the rainy season. Using his bare hands, Sondus carefully ripped off a branch. He then walked deeper into the jungle and came upon a Yobishka tree. He picked up a small, dry twig from the ground. He then made his way back to his hut, filled with an inexplicable cheerfulness.

Sondus was standing at the chief's door when he once again heard the crowing of a rooster with a seemingly distorted sense of time. He hesitated. It crowed two more times. Sondus returned to his room to wait. The sound seemed to him like a bad omen. He remembered the coconut water he had left in his room. He grabbed it quickly, but instead of returning to the chief's hut, he found himself heading toward the princess's. She was still sleeping when he opened the door. He sat next to her. The scent of her body had changed, strong yet still alluring. The sandalwood and Arab perfumes left no trace. He kissed her cheek, and she wrapped her arms around him. "I see you're ready," she said.

"Yes. I was on my way to the chief, but the rooster cried three times."

"Go now, and come back quickly to tell me what happened," she said with a smile.

Sondus left without glancing at her again. All the workers in the village had now left. As he neared the chief's hut he saw two elderly men. He stopped to greet them.

"Is it true you're taking the journey to God?" asked one of them.

"Yes."

"My brother asked me to bring him to you. He has something to tell you," he said.

Sondus stepped closer to the brother and shook his hand, looking intently at his face and his milky-white eyes.

"Don't go, son," the brother said. "No one has ever come back from this journey. The way to God only leads to the end."

"But the chief said I can get back my manhood."

The old man gripped Sondus's hand tighter, as if fearing he might run away. Sondus felt his compassion.

"It's true. Your manhood and spirit are in God's keep, but I'm talking about the journey back. It's impossible. You can't come back to live with the girl. I feel your pain, my boy. I too have lost people I love. My son, my daughter, and my daughter's husband. My daughter had recently married and she left me with a newborn child. That's another story we don't have time for. My brother lost his eldest son, who was the same age as mine. Our wives had given birth to them in the same week. Those evil hunters snatched them away, God knows where to. We know my daughter has died, and my guess is that they sold our sons to some ship. If they were here, they would be grown men, close to your father in age.

The man continued: "I have followed your story from the day you arrived and felt sorrow for you while the village laughed at you and called you delusional. I asked my brother to bring me here, because unlike me, he can see, though he can't hear very well. Our life has been very difficult, but we're wiser for it. We came to see you, to warn you. Don't dive into that well. You'll never find your way back."

He released Sondus's hand and reached for his brother's. They walked away, talking in hushed voices. Sondus followed them with his eyes until they disappeared between the village huts. He hesitated to move, the words of the old man racing in his mind. He willed himself on and stood in front of the large wooden door, holding the branch from a Mkunazi tree, the twig from a Yobishka tree, and the coconut water. He carried them in a basket made of palm leaves which he had taken from the princess's room. He no longer felt self-possessed, knowing the old man had no reason to lie to him.

He was telling the truth. I felt it in my heart. But if I want my body and spirit to become whole, I must go. Knock on his door and walk in. Listen to every word he says. There might be a way.

The chief offered him a chair next to where the snake lay, and handed him a jug of water and a wooden board with sliced mangoes, flies buzzing above them.

"The journey begins at the well. There's no spell to help you do this, but you must shed all your fear and do everything in your power not to let it in, or it will kill you, and your body will be found floating on the surface within days. Only the wise are able to do this. As they say, 'When a cat is afraid, it pounces.' The demon is Satan disguised as a dog. Satan's role is to prevent anyone from reaching God. God created Satan, and he could put an end to him if he wanted to. God also created prophets, and he could put an end to them, but he doesn't want to. People need prophets to be the voice of reason, to chase the devil away. I'm the prophet in this village, and I'm sharing with you all I know."

Sondus listened with all his senses to every word the chief had to say. He had heard a great deal about the Arab Prophet, but he still didn't know what exactly a prophet did. The image of the bare-chested, mango-loving chief who smiled constantly and played with his beard did not fit Sondus's image of a prophet. Yet he knew the chief could face the demon without the aid of a book or an army. Unable to shake the memory of what the blind man had said, he decided he would ask the chief about the journey back when the time was right.

"There is a spell that protects you from the demon. You must use it correctly, because the slightest mistake is certain death. You must be as cunning as a cat. The demon's attack will be vicious. As it approaches, stand firmly rooted in place. The demon will hesitate for a moment, and that is when you throw the branch from the Mkunazi tree, which will grow into a thorny thicket that surrounds you with darkness. The demon will not be able to move, and the thorns will pierce every part of its enormous body. It will bleed endlessly and feel a world of pain. You won't be able to see the demon, but you'll hear its cries, as powerful as the roar of a lion. But don't be fooled – it will catch up with you. It may take a day or two, but it will find you. The distance you cover in two days it can cover in a quarter of a day. Its wounds will heal and the meat on its bones will regenerate countless times. Its cry will turn into a terrifying laugh. Once it reaches your ears, you should know it is behind you, only two-and-a-quarter days away. That's when you spill the coconut water, which will turn into a vast ocean between you. The demon will drink until his stomach gives out, then a new stomach will grow, and it will continue in this vein until all the water is gone. Once its laugh reaches your ears once again, the world around you will quiver. This, once again, tells you the demon is two and a quarter days away from you. By then you will be the same distance away from the Creator's caves. Do not stop even for a second. Channel all your fear, hopelessness, uncertainty, and fatigue into the power of the cat. When the demon catches up with you, you must get very close to it and look it square in the eye, then you must throw the Yobishka twig. A fire will swallow up the entire thorny forest, and the fire will be swallowed up by the ocean. Your fire will die but the fire of God will illuminate all the caves, of which there are many: cave of the spirits, speech, the sun, the moon, fire, water, sand, air. There's a cave for every part of the body for all animals. You must then lie prostrate before God. There's no need to say who you are or what you want. Just be still, looking at the ground, until God speaks to you and says 'Stand up'. At this point you'll see the cave where God keeps the members severed by the hands of invaders. If only God had protected us before he retreated to the caves. You'll hear a voice calling your name, and you'll know which belongs to you."

Sondus heard the voice calling him by his real name, Nano, and felt the ghost of his missing part move, as though it were made of flesh and blood. *Let's take the journey to God*, whispered the ghost in Nano's ear.

"Will I be able to retrieve the princess's member? All the women in Unguja have theirs severed when they're children."

The chief hesitated to answer. He swatted away flies from a slice of mango and put it in his mouth.

"When you are kneeling before God, you can ask."

"How do I come back?" Sondus finally asked.

"Shawiri ya Mawjudu," began the chief. "All I can offer is our modest way of facing the demon. God will guide your return. You'll have a restored soul and body. God's ways are not the same as ours. You should know that many people who make this journey choose to remain with God. These are people who have lost faith in the life we live here, and who fear the evil other humans are capable of. Many villagers who journeyed to God to avoid enslavement didn't know how to combat the demon or their own fears, so they fell prey to the demon and became part of it, helping it grow more vicious and powerful. Those who managed to reach the caves safely have remained there. They are wandering souls. You, on the other hand, have a reason to return. I don't think you're willing to part with the Arab woman. It appears she feels the same way. Given the chance, I wouldn't give up my life on this earth, in this village. I think it's beautiful despite the difficulties. Only souls live alongside God – there are no men, women, children, or animals. They roam the air like clouds. If God were to take my soul to the caves, I would be content to do as God wills, but he created us for life on earth, not the life he lives."

The chief smiled. He looked around the hut as though searching for something. He picked up the mango plate again and ate a few pieces. Tugging at his beard, he pulled out a long hair that didn't belong to him. He knew which of his wives it belonged to based on its texture. He threw it aside and continued.

"Leave the Mkunazi branch and Yobishka twig and the coconut water with me. I'll prepare them for you. It's not an easy task – it will take me two weeks. That's all I can do for you. Now, go back to your girl. She's waiting for you."

THE PRISONERS STRIKE BACK

Sultan Suleiman bin Salim was not the least bit surprised when the British attacked Unguja on 27 August 1896. What became one of the darkest days of his life had started out quite ordinarily. Since throwing his personal servant Mutei in a cell, he missed him terribly in the mornings, especially since the servant who had replaced him wasn't as skilled at cleaning his blessed body.

That morning, he woke up to the sound of adhan, stretched his body, and tapped the shoulder of the woman who lay beside him so she could return to the harem. He tried to recall her name and whether she was the daughter of some wealthy merchant or a relative of his. He knew they'd been married for a while, but he just couldn't put a name to her, so he resorted to "Fatuma Jama". She got up, yawned, lazily put on her clothes, then gathered her colourful perfume bottles and various other objects and left. The servant then brought a steel basin, large enough to accommodate a mighty sultan arse capable of producing more than five pounds of excrement.

As soon as he sat on the basin, and his body relaxed and the urine began to flow, accompanied by a slight burning sensation from drinking too much ginger, the sultan heard the unmistakable sound of the British Maxim gun. When the palace shook as if from an earthquake, he bolted up in a panic. "The British!" he cried in the servant's face. "Damn them! Where are the fucking guards?"

When the palace was hit a second time moments later, the guards gathered around the sultan, lifted his naked body, and carried him to the basement, which had been constructed with this kind of emergency in mind by a brilliant architect whose name was unknown. He had designed many other palaces in India, East Africa, and other British colonies. If the palace were to topple to the ground, the basement was the safest place to be. The basement had been turned into a temporary prison a few years earlier on the sultan's orders, as he wanted to submit disobedient slaves to a punishment worse than death. A quick death would be merciful, he reasoned. He decided he would starve them, deprive them of sunlight, whip them, and then urinate on their wounds. He would turn them into living corpses. When they finally died, their bodies were to be fed to stray dogs and vultures. If they didn't die within two weeks, the guards were to kill them. The sultan was certain they were damned to an eternity in hell for rebelling against their master.

The young British consul still residing at the princess's palace had forewarned him, so the sultan was unsurprised by the attack, but he was shocked to find dozens of African prisoners - who had been sentenced to torture, decay, and imprisonment - apparently alive and well, though their colour was dull, their hair overgrown, and the clothes on their bodies had become tattered from humidity and the water from the ocean occasionally leaking into the basement. "Who are these people?" he demanded from the guards.

"They're the bodies you wanted to feed to stray dogs and vultures." The answer came from Mutei, who stood amid the crowd of prisoners.

"Get me away from here. Now!"

The Maxim gun sounded again, followed by a hail of bullets and the sound of the palace crumbling. The Englishman who was part of the British mission to Unguja burst into the basement. The sultan had taken him as a secret lover and invited him to live in the palace. It dawned on the sultan that the Englishman had been sent with the sole purpose of putting an end to his affairs with young captive natives; he was also there to spy on him and plot against him and his sultanate, and against Islam as whole.

A tall, thin prisoner – dull colour, thick hair, foul smell, sparks flying from his eyes – approached the sultan. Despite the sound of guns, his voice was loud and clear, close to a roar. "Do you recognise me?" he asked.

The sultan didn't respond and instead pretended to examine the ceiling.

Although the guards stepped in to drag the prisoner away, he managed to break away and get close enough to put his face to the sultan's. "Do you remember me?" he bellowed.

"I remember you."

"Do you remember what you did to me and my wife and children?"

"It was God's will," the sultan replied weakly. "You were my favourite slave. I believe I treated you well, but it was God's will."

"Today we'll show you what God's will is for you." He spat on the sultan's blessed face. The rest of the prisoners then descended on the sultan's large, naked body. They stripped the guards of their weapons but left them unharmed. After all, the guards had fed them and kept them alive for many years, knowing full well that the sultan would never come down to the prison; he didn't know the way, and in any case didn't think anyone who had been sent there was still alive.

The prisoners attacked the sultan haphazardly; they had never expected to find him among them. They struck him, spat on him. One prisoner yelled for the rest to hold him down so he could castrate him. The sultan howled with all his might, begging them not to, but the desperate prisoners had already made the decision. However, they didn't have any tools at hand. A poorly, elderly man proposed they use the back of a rifle. "Crush his genitals until they're flat on the stone floor," he said.

They did so without any regard for the sultan's age, his howling and moaning, or the diarrhoea that seeped out of his body. They left him on the ground writhing in pain.

Some thought about finishing him off, but the Englishman pleaded with them not to. "You've done enough," he said. "You've had your revenge. Don't kill him. The British need him alive."

Within twenty-five minutes, the gunfire ceased. Silence fell, broken only by the sultan's incessant wailing and the occasional curses he blurted out at the jubilant prisoners, who attributed their unexpected victory to divine intervention. Minutes later, guards from India, Sudan, and Britain entered the basement. The British guards exchanged a few words with the Englishman. They arrested the sultan's guards and took away the weapons, then they carried the sultan away, with the Englishman following behind. Before they left, they instructed the prisoners to get out while they could.

The sultan survived. He was saved by surgeons from the Indian military. They operated successfully on his genitals, and attached a small golden tube to his urethra to help him urinate and to prevent it from closing up in case of infection. They kept him under close observation and he healed within thirty days.

As was commonly known, the sultan lived for many years to come. He was born on 13 February in a year forgotten to all, and he lived until 12 January 1964 or thereabouts. He vanished without a trace, like a shadow at dusk. During this indeterminable period:

he killed 883 Africans, seven Omani Arabs, and twenty Yemenis;

he decimated all of Unguja's large mammals – giraffes, elephants, cheetahs, and lions;

he sold 2,779,670 women, children, and men;

he engaged in sexual intercourse with 300 captive women and ejaculated approximately 15 gallons of semen into their bodies;

he only had one daughter;

he was infatuated with boys and ejaculated about a gallon into African and impoverished Arab boys until he was blessed with the Englishman, who was experienced and beautiful, his skin fair and smooth. In his youth he had known many male lovers from high society, slave hunters, landowners, clove and ginger merchants, and sons of dignitaries, all of whom deposited their fluids into his behind, which later became the blessed arse of a sultan with tenuous connections to King Solomon;

he ate 70 tonnes of meat, vegetables and grains, and defecated 30 tonnes;

he urinated 10,000 litres with traces of uraemia;

he pillaged 805 villages and enslaved their inhabitants; and

he enslaved 90 per cent of Unguja's inhabitants.

These were some of the things he did before turning fifty-four.

Curiously, following the encounter with the prisoners, his life did change somewhat – not because he lost his vigour or found a conscience, but for other reasons related to shifts in the centres of power, the ambitions of the British and the

French, and the Germans' activities on the mainland. The change was related to the fact that he had suffered a bitter defeat because he was the weakest of all the players. There was a great deal to be learned from the British attack. That invasion triggered what was lauded in the international press and history books as the shortest war in history: the twenty-five-minute war waged by Britain against the army of Sultan Suleiman bin Salim.

When the sultan healed completely, the British sat with him to settle the scores. They explained their motivation for the attack, which he had already known and dismissed as illegitimate, unfair, and without any grounding in reality. He believed in the saying "If you're strong, you have no need for logic."

"Despite signing the treaty ending slavery on 5 June 1887, Your Highness has continued to deceive an international community fully devoted to the protection of human rights and to equality. You have failed to adhere to the terms stipulated in the treaty. We maintained constant surveillance around your vessels and discovered that they were full of Africans who had been captured, enslaved, and exploited for your personal gain. We have released all the prisoners, slaves and captives, all those who were coerced into labour, so restoring compliance with the provisions stipulated in the treaty which you have voluntarily signed.

"Your efforts to seek closer ties with the French enemy have been a concern for Great Britain, and a threat to the security and stability of the country as well as its colonies in

Asia, and to its ships in the Indian Ocean. You have allowed French spies to cross to the African mainland under your protection and care, and enabled them to control Mahayana and other strategic islands. You have given your blessings to the marriage of the Mahayanan queen to a French spy. Unguja has effectively become a part of France, a haven for its spies. We don't know the extent of your relationship with the Germans, who continue to move freely around the mainland, unfortunately spreading the Lutheran Protestant way among Africans."

"You have received multiple warnings from the consul against undermining Britain's security and violating human rights through your persistent engagement in the trading of slaves. You incited your people to take up arms against us. The sermon you recently delivered at the mosque was a betrayal. We now demand that you sign the protectorate treaty, which will allow you to remain the sultan indefinitely – but under the British crown and protection. No one will have the right to rob you of your throne, which is yours by right of inheritance, except by an order from the Queen of England, who safeguards the interests of all. This treaty will protect you against foreign powers, especially France and Germany, who covet your land and wealth. Britain will protect the people. It will civilise and help them prosper financially and culturally. It will respect the beliefs and religions of others, which some countries do not."

The sultan no longer felt any pain. He had recovered from his grave injuries and his appetite had returned. He was feeling mentally stable, having overcome a bout of recurring nightmares: attacks by prisoners, slaves, and animals, and strange creatures he had never seen; the ghost of Tippu Tip; his daughter drowning in a vast ocean. His recovery was thanks to the Indian surgeon and the psychologist who had been specially brought in from Britain and who had somehow convinced him to let go of the idea of revenge and to try to understand the motives behind the actions of those who had done harm to him, and even to try and find compassion and pray for them.

"I now understand your reasons for attacking our island," said the sultan, calmly addressing the British. "But I still have lingering questions that I believe I deserve an answer to. Firstly, have you freed the slaves everywhere else in the world? Have you brought back the Irish you sold to America in 1650? You'll never meet an Irish seaman who doesn't know this story. It is passed down from generation to generation. Have you freed the Africans and Asians who built the great British cities, ports, and roads, and worked the farms? Have you granted them rights? Have you made amends to their descendants? Did you think about the civilians when you fired your cannons at residential areas and the peaceful palaces of Unguja? Have you apologised to the people who—"

"Your Highness," the consul interrupted him, "the civilised world is free. There are no longer slaves or captives or people working under servitude, as is the case in Unguja. That belongs to the past, which we will never return to, thanks to the efforts of the free world represented by Britain and its allies. We would like to draw your attention to something important: Great Britain does not expect to be answering your questions, but rather expects your complete understanding and cooperation in order for you to preserve your personal and national interests. As aforementioned, you will remain the sultan, but under the British crown. There will be a designated governor appointed by Her Majesty, who will act as your adviser. The English leaders have thought long and hard about who will govern here. As you know, your kinsmen also aspire to rule and cooperate with us, but we trust you and we want to benefit from your extensive experience in administration. My advice to you is to avoid unhelpful questions and issues that have already been dealt with. An astute politician always starts from the present moment, not from the past, and reads history only for entertainment and not to settle scores with people who have long been buried underground."

"Understood," the sultan said after a brief silence.

"Please read the protectorate agreement. There is a Swahili version so you can understand it before you sign. You will see that it contains many benefits for you and your country, while also preserving the interests of Great Britain."

"I don't need to understand it, I will sign it right away." The sultan maintained a veneer of composure, but the underlying anger was palpable to all in attendance.

"This is a very encouraging start," said the consul with a smile. "We appreciate your understanding and confidence in Great Britain and the Queen, who personally has carefully reviewed this agreement. Her Majesty's greatest concern was to preserve your national interests, as well as those of Britain. Well, please sign the agreement, and I'll then explain it to Your Majesty in detail, word for word."

THE BLIND PRISONERS

When the prisoners emerged from the palace's basement, they were met with a blazing sun that beat down on them. They were all, except Mutei, naked and barefoot, their eyes swollen and nearly blind. With a hand between their legs to shield themselves from the gaze of passers-by, and the other hand on their foreheads to protect them from the sun, they walked closely behind Mutei to a destination they had all agreed on: whichever house, hut, or cave the singer Uhuru lived in.

They were worn out. The exhaustion had seeped into their joints, but what pained them most was walking on the scorching ground with their bare feet, which had become tender after spending years in a dark and humid prison. So they walked on the tips of their toes, taking cover under the shade of walls and trees along the way. They encountered no other people; the streets were deserted. Elsewhere, wealthy locals were clutching their chests, waiting expectantly, and a number of British troops were scattered across different areas.

The sultan had ignored the consul's warning and disregarded his British lover's advice two days prior: "Call on the British consul immediately and ask for Unguja to be placed under Great Britain's protection – you have much to gain." He had spoken in a whisper about the planned attack. He had told him that the British were serious and under pressure; they were in a feverish race with the French, who might beat them to the attack. The British didn't want to enter a war with the French over a little island whose only importance was its strategic location.

Still, the sultan had not expected the British to bombard the palace where he lived. He'd imagined marines inching toward the island, surrounding it perhaps, which would have led to negotiation and compromise using peaceful diplomatic rhetoric and the logic of shared interests. Not this brutal dialogue of cannons, this destruction of the centre of power with him, his women, servants, and young men still inside.

Many Ungujans escaped into the jungle, but some remained. The sultan's guards didn't put up much of a fight; they gave themselves over in a state of shock. Thus, the first people to emerge onto the streets were the wretched prisoners, the sun searing their feet, heads, eyes, and bare bodies. They didn't know which direction to take, but Mutei did; he knew where Uhuru's hut was.

Eyes might have been watching the prisoners from behind bars, wanting to know what had come over the town. Some thought the prisoners were strange creatures brought by the ships that shelled the island. Some thought they were jinn, or cannibals, or sorcerers showing off their immunity to the gunfire. Others reasoned that their naked bodies, their strange gait, the odd look in their eyes, and the fact that they were hiding from the sun indicated that they were zombies. But why would the British bring zombies with them? And where was Mutei, the personal servant to the sultan whom everyone knew, taking them?

Mutei and Uhuru had never spoken; they came from very different worlds, and the only thing they had in common was their Africanness. Mutei was one of the obedient servants whose hearts never spoke of revolution, so totally were they dominated. Their servitude was grounded on a number of holy sayings attributed to the Arab Prophet. They would go to heaven if they behaved as good slaves. Uhuru, on the other hand, was one of few the masters couldn't tame. She sang and danced as she pleased. Masters either feared her, pretended she didn't exist, or decided no good could come of her, which meant no good could come from between her legs.

The prisoners were on their way to Uhuru, the only woman on the island to have a home that belonged to her. It was on the coast. Even those who knew where her house was never found her there. Her house was part of her legend. She was the only Ungujan not to have any ties to the slave trade. She made her living from passers-by who enjoyed watching her, and was as free as the wind and the seagulls that crowded the skies.

We should go and find her, should we not?

They walked through what was once a market buzzing with buyers and sellers. There was no one there. The dogs that had once gathered at the butcher's ran away on hearing the cannons and occupied the abandoned buildings and sewers and the jungle nearby. The market was silent save for the whispers of female slaves inside a row of structures made of reeds. They were temporary holding cells for females and eunuchs, where they were fattened to become more beautiful and their bodies rubbed with coconut oil. They were sometimes marked with fake signs of smallpox to convince the buyers that they were no longer prone to that dangerous disease, which allowed sellers to ask for a higher price. The prisoners heard shouting and wailing, occasionally laughing, coming from the women. They walked through an open field full of Christ's thorn trees and dried grass, a short distance from the river. It was used to bury human remains and the rotting flesh of animals – carcasses of donkeys, dogs, and cats. There were bodies disintegrating in the open. The smell was foul. Small thorns, the fruit of burweed, were scattered on the sandy, rocky, chalky ground. They pricked the prisoners' feet, making it difficult for them to advance. Mutei, being the only one whose sight was clear, took to removing thorns from their feet. He was protected by the leather shoes he wore, and from the shame of nakedness by the once-luxurious, now-filthy clothes he'd had on before he was thrown in prison.

The prisoners climbed a small hill made of sand and stones. At the top, Mutei was able to identify the direction of the hut. It was to the east of the hill, a short distance away, near a large headland.

It took the exhausted prisoners two hours to cover a distance that usually took Uhuru thirty minutes. Finally, they stood before the small hut made of chalky stone, mud, and reeds.

The hut stood under the shade of the large headland, about a mile long, which extended into the ocean. The remains of tall seasonal plants swayed in the gentle breeze that smelled of salt and fish. Nothing was growing save the abundant, wilted Mkunazi trees. It was socially and legally prohibited to cut them down because of mythical stories surrounding them. Some considered them one of the trees of heaven. Not far from the hut, at the cove of the headland, stood a boabab tree, like a sailing ship drowning between the rocks.

White chalk had been painted over the hut's exterior. There were drawings of African villagers dancing, and women carrying baskets of fruit and pots of water on their heads. There were drawings of slaves with heavy, steel chains around their necks and legs, a white man walking behind them with a large pipe in his mouth and a long whip in his hand. A low fence made of rocks surrounded the hut. It had a small door made of wood and iron. The door had been left ajar.

It seemed to the prisoners that there were people in the hut. There were footprints on the sand, and faint voices coming from within, as though coming from under the ground. The prisoners stood at the gate, bleary eyes struggling to see, shifting their weight from one foot to the other.

Mutei hesitated before calling out, "Jambo. Jambo."

The voices inside fell silent. The whispering of the wind caressing the sand and rocks was the only sound that remained.

"Jambo jambo," he called again.

"Jambo sana," a feminine voice answered from inside.

A pause.

"Karibu, karibu." the voice added welcomingly,

Mutei stepped ahead of the remaining ten naked, jaundiced, thick-haired, bleary-eyed prisoners. They followed as if under the influence of a drug. A sharp sound filled the air. The door to the hut opened. When they walked in, they were surprised to find the hut totally empty. They glanced around the rectangular room, as humid and full of stagnant air as the basement but with plenty of light coming in through the door. On the walls they saw similar drawings to the ones outside. There were carved stones. Animal leather hung on the walls, emitting a foul smell. There were old Arab leather shoes and fish hung up to dry. The floor was spotless. A colourful, Arab-style mat made of palm leaves lay on the ground. In one corner, there were drums with three legs commonly seen in Unguja, and two wooden drumsticks placed over them. These were all the musical instruments Uhuru had.

The prisoners were not naive enough to think the hut was empty. They felt the sensation of being watched, like the sting of the sun.

"Jambo jambo," called Mutei anxiously.

They heard the sharp sound once again. One of the leather pieces on the wall moved, revealing Uhuru's beautiful face. As usual, she was wearing nothing but the goatskin loincloth around her waist, the same colour as her skin. She recognised Mutei and asked about his companions.

"They were imprisoned underground. Now they have nowhere to go. So we came here."

"Many before them have come here. Come in," Uhuru said ruefully.

They stepped through a small opening behind the piece of leather, which required them to crouch down. They found themselves in a vast room with dozens of people, young and old. It was like an endless passage, but it soon became obvious, given the moisture and the smell of the air and the sound of waves, that the room led to the beach. Uhuru later told them that, at certain times of the year, the cries of slaves could be heard there. Perhaps this was where the pirates kept them before shipping them away. Perhaps it was where they stayed, or they used it to store other stolen goods.

"We're the children of this land," Uhuru said. "Yet we hide away in caves while the invaders live in palaces. There is a limit to everything."

"Yes," replied two prisoners. "There is a limit to everything."

"The British will end Arab rule on the island," said Mutei.

"The British are worse," replied Uhuru, smiling uncertainly. "And the Germans are even worse. They all want to take over our land, and they won't hesitate to kill if they feel that their interests are threatened. We must end the rule of Arabs and British and whoever else ourselves. It looks like the sultan has now surrendered."

A prisoner coaxing out a thorn from his foot cried, "We castrated him!"

"What do you mean, you castrated him?"

"We flattened his genitals on the ground using the back of a rifle. He'll probably die as a result. If he lives, he'll be lucky if he can even piss," said Mutei.

Uhuru was incredulous and couldn't resist a smile. "You castrated the sultan himself?"

"Yes," an older man replied. "And we knew it was the sultan and not his ghost because of his screams. A ghost can't scream or shit on the ground like he did."

Once the wave of laughter subsided, the prisoners were asked to relay the story in all its detail, and they complied. Everyone surrounded them, listening intently.

"We heard you had died after being tortured and after the sultan had personally pissed on each of your bodies," said one of the women.

"If it weren't for Mutei, who'd had the guards feed us, we would all be dead. The guards were with the people. They belong to our tribes. Two were relatives of mine. The sultan didn't know that. He didn't even know where the prison was."

Another woman approached a prisoner and stood close to him. "You are Juma Comba, aren't you?" she said.

"Yes," he said.

She stepped even closer. "You were one of the sultan's guards."

"Yes," he said, his voice quivering.

"You killed my husband," the woman screamed, and leapt at him. "You killed him with your bare hands. I'm going to kill you. When I heard you had died I was elated. I thought maybe God was fair after all. But here you are, standing among us, and I have to kill you."

People stepped in to separate them. They pulled the prisoner out from beneath her nails and teeth.

"Forgive me," murmured Juma Comba repeatedly. "I was a wretched slave. I had no will of my own. I was ordered by the sultan to carry out the execution. Forgive me. The sultan executed my wife and children too. We were his victims. Please forgive me."

The woman fell to her knees and sobbed. Uhuru pulled her into her arms, whispering to her until she calmed down.

Others chimed in:

"The real killer is the sultan. Juma was forced to carry out an order. There was no animosity between him and your husband."

"He killed my husband. I saw it with my own eyes. Everyone saw."

"It is the sultan who must pay the price for what happened to your husband," said Uhuru sternly. "Not this poor man. Him, you must forgive. He is brother and kin to you."

Later on, in less than two years, life presented yet another unexpected twist. The woman married the man who had killed her husband, vindicating the strange notion that out of the ashes of hatred, love can arise.

With a wooden lever usually used in boatbuilding, Uhuru effortlessly lifted a large rock and placed it at the entrance of the cave. This allowed her to keep a close eye on the outer area. Mutei and the prisoners finally understood why none of the vile men who had their way with anyone their hearts desired, meaning every woman and every boy on earth, were able to catch Uhuru in her hut. It had become clear how she evaded the seamen who encountered her at the market and followed her back to her hut, only to find that she had vanished inside without a trace. They would return dismayed and disturbed, and when asked would invent a story, adding new dimensions to Uhuru's legend, while she withdrew into the depths of her cave, safe and sound.

Uhuru's father was a fierce village chief and sorcerer. Her ancestors had been the first to resist the Portuguese invasion of the African mainland, hundreds of years before. Ultimately, her ancestors submitted to Portuguese rule and adopted Christianity instead of the magic they had practised for generations. They began to love Christ the way the Portuguese taught them to. When the Portuguese were driven out by the Omanis, they gradually abandoned Christianity and returned to their pagan traditions, though they preserved many Catholic everyday practices.

The dancer had been brought up within a blend of different cultures. She had some knowledge of the holy book, but her ancestors had left the strongest mark on her character.

She learned from her father how to be independent and free, and how to guard that freedom: not by being passive and forgiving but with cunning, force, and magic. As her father had taught her, "All prophets are good, but their followers are evil. To live among the followers, you must be far more evil and wicked."

Her father had been killed during the long wars with Tippu Tip and his soldiers, who were armed to the teeth with spears that shot fire. A staggering number of Uhuru's people were captured, but she managed to escape to the jungle, where she remained a while, a beast among beasts, until one day she decided to return to Unguja, the den of evil, pledging to live freely, in honour of her father.

She had first appeared at the Friday market soon after Islamic prayers had concluded, on the road leading to the slave quarter. She was seen playing the drums and dancing erratically, barely dressed, and singing:

> I am the sorcerer, daughter of Satan
> Come near me and meet your end
> I emerged from hell, and to hell I will return.

No one dared touch her. Ungujans believed in sorcery more than they believed in God. Slave hunters estimated a very high price for Uhuru and longed to capture her. She was a fortune running loose, with no master to claim her. The vilest men lusted. They conjured her up in their dreams and caressed themselves to the rhythm of her body.

Uhuru herself dreamt of freedom for her people; of ruling the nation; of leading an army; of defeating the enemy and getting back the land. She never uttered a word of this to anyone, but she alluded to it the day Mutei and his companions sought refuge with her and in her cave.

"Our people are free. We have been free since the day God created us. The journey before us is long and, like all journeys, it begins with intention, with a sense of conviction. When you take the first step, you will have arrived."

These simple words ignited the spark of revolution, though it did not take place until 1964, years after Uhuru had died. It was around her hut that the first African neighbourhood inhabited by emancipated slaves and lower-class Arab immigrants was formed. It was named after her: Uhuru, meaning *freedom*.

RUIN

Life in Unguja came to a standstill once British forces arrived and declared the slaves free. Servants left their posts at once. Early-rising bakers who stood before blazing ovens every day to make the masters' bread left the dough in its wooden bowls and the fire burning and walked out. Metalsmiths, blowers of the forge, makers of swords, knives, pots, and pans, as well as the chains that shackled their own bodies, rose from the wooden chairs that had become part of them. They removed the chains from their waists and feet and walked out. Potters left behind compost and clay, and brickmakers abandoned their brick ovens by the river and walked away with their hands and feet still covered in mud. Millers whose rough hands fed the entire town, whose nails were long and filthy, who worked with empty stomachs, bloody hands, and lungs full of flour dust and who often succumbed to a slow death from an incurable lung disease – they too hauled their weary bodies and walked out, covered in a layer of flour.

Waste collectors left the rubbish rotting in place. The masters' excrement overflowed zinc buckets and streamed along the ground. No one was there to collect and bury the waste in some faraway place. Armies of insects descended upon it. The town that had once smelled of sandalwood, cloves, and frankincense now reeked of perpetual decay.

There was no one to bury the dead. The job required digging through solid ground with an axe, and who but a servant would do that? It was for the masters to die and be buried in graves that waited to receive them, and for their bodies to be prayed over by other masters.

The Indian jewellers were without work; the forge blowers had unshackled themselves. Monkeys played on abandoned farms. Deer and rabbits nibbled away at the ground. The labourers who had been worked to the bone had gone.

Who will sell the vegetables?

Who will prepare the food?

Who will fetch fresh water from the well or river?

Who will break their backs carrying basic necessities?

Who will clean the masters' shoes?

Who will sew and wash and iron their clothes?

Who will cut their hair?

Who will rid them of lice?

Who will accompany the children to play, and wait in excruciating boredom?

Who will sing and dance to liven up the masters' nights?

Who will feed the donkeys?

Who will walk all the distance to the jungles to fetch wood?

Who will butcher the meat?

There was no meat to eat, in any case. The animals were roaming freely. The plantations were neglected and desolate. Only poor Arab plantation managers and their aggrieved assistants remained. Whips made of hippopotamus hide, bamboo, and stalk were hanging limply from their hands, no longer able to threaten the good-for-nothing slaves.

The iron chains, hammers, anvils, clubs, and straps that used to torture and discipline now rang sadly in the corner.

Fishing boats stopped going out to sea and remained on the beach, allowing gulls, pelicans, and cats to feast on the rotten fish that still hung inside.

The creatures of the ocean slept soundly without knowing what had changed.

The deer and rabbits enjoyed a respite from traps yanking them by the limbs, knives grating against their skin, and teeth grinding their meat.

Fruit rotted on tree branches.

The bodies of the enslaved women could finally rest. No longer did they have to wash away the filth of every encounter before another one began, or to feign affection for every father, son, grandfather, and guest who demanded it.

Monkeys and squirrels ate freely, without sneaking around, without the sound of the guards' whistles or their murderous arrows.

Enslaved servants could finally stop saying the word "master". They were their own masters.

Buildings lay in heaps of rubble.

The grand mosques became dumping grounds. The devout masters believed in the holy saying "Cleanliness is a sacred act," but it was only the servants who cleaned.

Darkness fell. Lanterns no longer burned oil.

Masters were soiled and foul-smelling, reeking of sweat, lice rejoicing on their scalps.

Filth would have overtaken the entire island were it not for the British governor who ordered the sultan to create a public health department, and to hire emancipated slaves and pay them a monthly wage, which would come from taxpayers and from his healthy private reserves. It was the impression of the British that the sultan's wealth was outrageous and that he had hidden an absurd amount of gold and Maria Theresa thalers in a place known to him and no one else.

The number of thieves, beggars, sorcerers, and false prophets multiplied.

People didn't know what to do with their new-found freedom, so they wandered aimlessly in the empty markets, the filthy streets, and the dumping grounds. They walked the length of the port, which had turned into barracks abuzz with Indian, Sudanese, and British soldiers, and others from places Great Britain occupied. They spent their days in their new-found paradise dancing, eating, and drinking copiously.

After a month of doing as they pleased, urinating where they used to work, and stealing everything they could get their hands on – either for revenge, hunger or the restoration of justice – the emancipated slaves grew weary with the weight of their freedom. Their skills were no longer of use anywhere. There was no way to earn a living. All means of production belonged to the masters: every plantation, every boat, all the mango and clove trees, even the jungles and the fallow land, the beaches, the oceans, the rivers, every outlet in the market and in the centre of town, all the homes, palaces, all the land, every animal that wandered the streets, all the cattle, every method of hunting – the masters had owned everything. Until the British arrived and took over.

The land the slaves had been born on, which their ancestors had passed down, was now monopolised by the invaders. The slaves themselves became mere currency. The law had set them free, but it hadn't given them back their land nor compensated them for what they had lost.

Desperation led some to plead with their previous masters to hire them in exchange for money, or food and lodging, but the masters turned them away, earnestly believing it was a matter of time before slavery was re-established – the sultan had secretly promised them that it would be.

Be patient. Soon the British will beg us to get them working again. It's to their benefit, first of all, and for the sake of stability.

The masters were not much better off than the emancipated slaves. They too were suffering. They had in their safekeeping some grains and dried foods. Many had reserves of smoked meat. They had flour, oil, wood, and coal, spices, sugar, ghee, herds of cattle, and chickens. But they didn't know how flour was made into bread. Some didn't even know how to light a fire using Yobishka twigs in the absence of matches. They had all the riches, yet they grew hungry and filthy, flies surrounding them, disease ravaging them. Hair unkempt, beards overgrown, stomachs empty, faces ashen, eyes wandering – they became ghosts.

Some sold their land for very little money to Indian buyers who were caught in the middle. Some pawned their land to these buyers, intending to take it back once the British decided to repeal the emancipation decree in a matter of months. Many were certain beyond a shadow of a doubt that it was in the interest of the British to do so. When they failed to pay on time, their land no longer belonged to them and was handed over to the Indian debtors.

Women and children of the lower classes were worse off. Once they exhausted their food reserves, they had to dig through heaps of rubbish on street corners to find something to eat – a piece of fruit, if they were lucky. They went to the river to bathe and to catch fish, where their children mixed with the children of the enslaved for the first time. Their interactions were often fraught. Language was a storm waiting to unleash itself. The children of the master class had no name for the children of the slave class except "servant". Nothing about that struck them as unusual, whereas slaves and their children couldn't stand it. They wanted to be considered citizens, as the law decreed them. The master class saw themselves as the citizens. Their grandparents were born on this land, and they had brought it out of the darkness of ignorance into the light of civilisation. They wanted the natives to precede their names with "sir" and "madam". The natives refused to do that. Battles, large and small, ensued: along the river, by the rubbish heaps, in the dilapidated market, on the coast, in the nearby jungles. Wherever people gathered, language added fuel to the fire. The town was descending into chaos. The economy collapsed. Life came to a halt. Until an Anglo-Sultan decree was introduced:

Every emancipated worker is entitled to return to their post, wherever it may be, and it is the responsibility of the employer to remunerate them in cash on a monthly, weekly, or daily basis, according to the enclosed schedule.

The decree stated that anyone who violated the order would have their means of production and land confiscated, which would then be managed by the state or a representative. Offenders might also face prison charges, be sent to exile, or be sentenced to hard labour in the tropical forests in one of Britain's colonies.

Only then did life resume its movement, albeit with difficulty and much hesitation. The masters couldn't take the insolence of the former slaves and their show of freedom. They refused any instructions put to them, no matter how tactfully they were worded. There were still no mutually agreed-upon words to describe the unprecedented situation. It was a new way of life; the birth of the emancipated slaves and the death of the system that had enslaved them. The language of days past had also to die, and a new one would need to arise from its ashes, the former having failed completely as a tool of communication.

The emancipated slaves returned to work, but they wouldn't work long hours. They left when they grew tired, didn't show up when it didn't suit them, and refused to be scolded. They no longer had to work as long as they had enough money to pass the day at home, or at one of the drinking venues that proliferated on the island and where many women from humble backgrounds earned their living in sex work. The master learned to avoid scolding the workers, particularly if they showed up to work with stomachs full of local liquor, lest he receive a brutal beating that left him unconscious or have his face spat upon for the crime of living in the past.

Some freed slaves took to enjoying long periods of rest in the middle of the workday, perhaps taking a drink and drawing their fellow workers into a dance. The meaning of freedom took many different forms. For some, freedom meant chaos, rebellion, and disregard. For others, it meant revenge and nothing more. It meant obstructing the masters' ways and going against their every word. The worst phenomenon of this era was the looting. Some freed slaves believed that anything the invaders owned in fact belonged to them. They took it back whenever an opportunity arose. Even the British were looted, which led the consul to address it as a matter of ethics. He believed that the problem was a lack of a moral compass, and that the solution was to take up a faith and follow its rules. Islam wasn't an option for many. The British administration had linked the practice of enslavement with the faith of the previous rulers, the sultan chief among them, which made many Muslims abandon their faith.

A big church was built. Then a school for children and adolescents. The aim was to get the emancipated slaves closer to God, and to teach them not to steal, commit adultery, tell lies, or drink alcohol. To show them how to forgive.

The sultan had never built any schools. The fact that he spread Islam didn't mean he taught good principles and work ethics. He once said to his Arab Muslim ministers, in a rare moment of clarity, "We have not done justice to the teachings of Islam. For that, we must answer to God on Judgement Day. We spread Islam as far as we could, but we didn't practise it in our own lives. We didn't forgive or show mercy. Life lured us away, and here we are today. As the Arabs of Andalusia one day awoke to the sword of the Franks, we awoke to the sound of the Maxim gun having failed God's test." He stopped short of telling them that he had paid the price with his body, that God had wanted to teach him a lesson.

There was nothing the sultan could do to halt the missionary work of the British. Unlike the church, he wasn't offering anyone food, clothes, or shelter. People were beginning to see those offerings as little miracles. When the sultan complained to the consul, the latter replied, "Don't you believe in religious freedom? Did anyone stand in your way when you were spreading the word of Islam? At least the Christian missionaries are not spending the country's money. Instead, they spend the donations of generous believers from around the world. It's important to us that the citizens are guided by morals, regardless of which religion they practise. After all, Islam and Christianity come from the same root. They spread the teachings of Prophet Moses. If you want to share Islam's teachings with the world, we will not stand in your way."

Following the advice of people close to him who worried about the sultanate and its future, the sultan didn't utter another word on the matter. The British wouldn't remain on the island forever. As soon as they left, the natives would revert to their original faith. After all, people follow the faith of their kings.

The church's teachings left many unmoved. Whenever support waned and people got hungry, they lost their faith in the words of Prophet Moses. They lied, stole, killed, and committed adultery. The only thing that deterred them was the penal law copied from India, which was clear, comprehensive, tough, and oppressive: He who is not deterred by the judgement of the Lord shall be disciplined by the rod of mankind.

People began to escape to the mainland, towards the mother jungle, especially after an incident where a group of emancipated slaves practised what they called their freedom by robbing a clove merchant. When he fought back, they beat him and stabbed him several times with poisoned knives, and he instantly died. The British military court sentenced them to death by hanging. The execution happened in plain sight. Everyone gathered to see. That's when they realised that the British were no more merciful than their old masters. Some who understood what freedom meant in those circumstances remained, and adhered to the boundaries of their freedom. Others either fled as far away as possible, sought remnants of their tribe, or crossed the gulf to the African mainland. Some joined what was later called the First Liberation Camp, under the leadership of the singer Uhuru in her cave on the coast.

NOTHING CAN STAND
IN A LOVER'S WAY

It became clear to everyone in the village that the relationship between Sondus and the princess was sexual, and they were appalled. Why couldn't they wait for Sondus to take the princess back to her father and ask for her hand in marriage? Her father would likely accept, seeing as – at least according to word that travelled from Unguja – he was no longer the mighty sultan he had been. He was now a miserable eunuch. A puppet in the hands of the British. Those who were fond of exaggerating said he was going where the British told him, doing what the British told him, and bending over when the British told him. He was afraid of suffering the same fate as the people on the mainland, in the Congo, who had been obliterated at the hands of the Germans and Belgians. Given all that, why wouldn't the sultan marry his daughter to Sondus, who had gallantly regained his freedom? Wasn't it enough that his daughter was happy and safe? Perhaps she'd even give birth to an heir who would inherit the sultan's tattered throne and restore the glory of his ancestors.

"You can't do that here! The chief told me to tell you," the chief's wife blurted out. She had been sent by her husband when he could no longer ignore the villagers' complaints.

Sondus decided to hide away in his hut until the whispers died down, but then an old woman publicly confronted the chief. He was backed into a corner.

"How can we let such an abomination occur in our village? A man has taken a woman captive and continues to violate her in our midst. This will surely bring down the wrath of God upon our people. Like a raging storm, it will wipe the two of them from the face of the earth. It will snatch their souls and cast them into the distant, dark oceans until the end of time. Two people without organs practising sex – if there's ever a sign for the end of the world, this would be it!"

Now God had been brought into it, everyone had to sit up and wait for God's verdict, spoken through his messenger. So many people claimed to be his messengers, but when he wished to speak, he did so through a select few, among whom was the chief. But the chief was busy preparing the fetish for Sondus's journey. Besides, he had no answers for anyone, so he did what he could: he sent his wife to warn the deviants.

Then nature interfered and things took a turn for the worse. A gathering of eagles with enormous wings and beaks and long, twisted necks began to hover above the village. Their terrifying cries sent cats and dogs scattering in all directions. Goats bleated desperately; cows frantically sought shelter; farmers and hunters hurried to take cover in their homes with their children and elderly and to seek the village chief's protection, without whom they would be lost.

A spontaneous procession assembled, moving towards the chief's hut. When passing by Sondus's hut, the village singer improvised a song that heightened the dread in everyone's hearts.

> The strangers must die
> Yes, they must be killed
> And fed to the eagles
> Before the eagles feed
> On the flesh of our children
> Our own flesh and blood
>
> The cursed woman
> The cursed boy
> Half-souls both
> Bad omens both
>
> Here come the eagles
> Spreading their wings
> To stifle the living
> To stifle the dead
> Their claws sharp as rakes
> They need to devour

> Devour the children
> Devour the men
> Devour our creatures
> Devour the living
>
> Let the strangers die instead
> Here and now

Sondus burst out of his hut to find the princess, to protect her or at least die with her. He knew the villagers meant every word they said, and that the princess knew it too.

The villagers obstructed his way. But the chief's voice rose, imploring everyone to settle down.

"Anyone who kills will be killed. Anyone who kills an outsider will be killed, along with one of their siblings. Yes, the boy and the girl are cursed. The sky has told us so by sending these eagles. God speaks through his creations. If the word is good, God delivers it through the good prophets and chiefs. If the word is bad, God delivers it through the most despicable of his creatures. My people, you are well aware that killing a villain means their soul attaches itself to you for eternity. The soul penetrates your body. It sees through your eyes. It devours your tongue. You become more wicked than a demon. Your body will smell like decayed flesh. You'll be incapable of doing any good. Your heart will speak only of evil."

When the chief finished talking, the people fell silent and let go of Sondus, who stood bewildered in the middle of the crowd. The chief instructed him to come to his hut and bring the princess with him. Sondus did as he was told, leaving the crowd outside the chief's hut singing terrible songs, the village singer at the helm with a curiously fearful expression on her face. Eyes were fixed on the eagles flying overhead, anticipating their attack. Youngsters fetched their traditional weapons; the elders set tree branches on fire, hoping to disorient the eagles with the smoke; musicians brought giant drums and walked around the village beating them, followed by children, who were followed by their anxious mothers, who were followed by the village singer, the village's protector from harm.

"You must go together. It's no longer an option for the princess to stay here. We can't take her to her father for another half-month, and something might happen to her in the meantime. I suggest you take her with you. That way she too can restore her soul. And if you want, you could stay there with God, or come back from the caves – it's your choice. You can decide when you are standing before God. The mind is clearest then, as clear as dew. The heart is free of fear. The eye can see what it couldn't previously see, the past and the future."

"But I'm Muslim. The faqih taught me that God lives in the sky, not on earth. He sits on a throne—" said the princess.

"What are you talking about? What thrones are there in the sky?"

"Oh, I don't know. The faqih told me God's throne is like my father's, but much greater. Then he took it back and said it's beyond our capacity as humans to imagine what it looks like. All I know is that God lives in the sky and sits on a throne."

"So God is very far away. And it's impossible to reach him. Isn't that right?" said the chief with a smile.

"I don't know," the princess said, smiling back. "God was always by my father's side, granting him every wish. But now it sounds like he abandoned him for the British."

"God is from this land. He's not made of air, so he doesn't dwell in the sky. He lives in caves. God created himself from the same clay he created us from. This is what our grandfathers have taught us. The Portuguese tried to teach us otherwise. They said God had a son whom he sent to earth from the sky, then he sent him up again after humans crucified him. But we saw with our own eyes how their God let the helpless natives die. Then the Arabs said God had no son or wife, and they tried to convince us he is just and merciful. But they began to sell us and send us overseas, to castrate our men and hold our women captive, and to slaughter the elephants. We knew then that they knew nothing about God."

"All I know is that I'll follow Sondus wherever he goes. Even if he goes to the caves. It doesn't matter which God we find. I'll go with him no matter what."

"Nothing can stand in a lover's way," said the chief as he added something to the coconut water.

The princess smiled, and Sondus discreetly placed his hand on her back. "Nothing can stand in a lover's way," he said.

"I need some time alone to finish this fetish. Go to your hut. I'll bring you the fetish when it's done."

At the door, the princess asked, "Isn't it a bad idea for us to be in the same hut together?"

Sondus reached for her warm thin hand. "Only an hour or so left and the journey to God begins," he said.

No one was outside the hut. The eagles had been chased away by the smoke and the drums. They could be seen in the far distance, like a murmuration of starlings.

Taking a turn, Sondus and the princess spotted the two old men from earlier in the story. The brothers rose to their feet and greeted them.

"My brother and I are here to tell you again. Don't go to the cave, son. We beg of you. We're your elders. Believe us."

Sondus pressed the blind man's large, dry hand. "We've already decided, Father. We're going to restore our souls and get rid of this curse that follows us wherever we go."

"If you go, you'll never come back. They mean you harm. The chief doesn't know this. Or he knows and is pretending not to know. He can't refuse what the people want. And he can't contradict the prophecy of the village singer, that cunning woman. The people have made up their minds. As for the eagles, well, they have to fly somewhere. Why shouldn't they fly above our village? And the depravity the people are so outraged by – the village is full of it. There's a sinner in every home. You two have committed a grievous sin, but who among us hasn't? There's a man in this village who slept with his brother's wife every time her husband went away. The village singer didn't foresee the brother's death. Do you know why? Because she's the brother's wife! Children, we don't have much time. Don't go into the well. Take the road to the coast instead. It's a path full of thorny bushes, but your donkey is capable enough. If you're lucky, you'll encounter fishermen who will take you to the island of Pemba, which isn't too far from here. From there you can go to Unguja or Mombasa. Unguja is not as you left it. The sultan, your father, is powerless. Even goats disregard him. The British have taken over. He's a ghost of a person, a shadow of a ghost. But Mombasa is a big city. You can do whatever you please. It's a godless city, as we all know. But if you climb down that well, it'll be the end of you. You won't find a dog, let alone a God. The singer needs her prophecy to come true so people continue to believe in her. Our forefathers used to say, 'If the house of trust is shattered, nothing can put it back together.' People think everything will fall apart once people lose faith in the all-knowing village singer. She doesn't share a prophecy unless she's absolutely certain of it. I beg you. I beg you not to enter the well. Let her prophecy fail this time so you can save yourselves. Let me say it more plainly: she needs a victim so she can get away with her sins. If God accepts your blood, she evades his curse and so does the village. Do you understand what I'm telling you?"

Sondus, whose mind was scrambling to find something to say in response, said, "We'll think about it, Father. We'll consider what you said very seriously. Be well."

"May I touch the princess's hand?"

The old man extended his hand and the princess leaned down softly and printed a kiss on it. Without meaning to, two tears fell from her eyes and flowed like a mythical stream over his coarse skin. Having spent an eternity braiding palm fronds into ropes, the smell still lingered on his hands. It took the princess back to Unguja, to the part of the market where straw mats, baskets, and textiles were sold. His old heart pounded faster as her warmth and tears seeped into him. He pulled his hand back. Without uttering a word, he turned around and anxiously reached for his brother's hand instead. They walked away, their voices fading gradually.

DEPARTURE

The fading crescent moon timidly announced the arrival of a new month. Darkness descended and the trees became giant ghosts rocking back and forth in the breeze. The plaintive cries of the spotted hyenas echoed in the distance as Sondus and the princess prepared their donkey for departure. There was no one in sight except the chief, offering his last words of guidance. Two days earlier, he had accompanied them to the well, both in the morning and at night. He was eager for them to avoid making any mistakes. He had even climbed down into the well himself to put Sondus and the princess at ease, using the rusted ladder the Portuguese had placed there hundreds of years ago during their bloody passage across the land. It was said that the Portuguese had sought to explore claims by villagers that God resided inside the well and that God had granted them an enormous amount of raw gold to turn them away, so they had left satisfied.

"Leave the donkey there. If you don't come back when

you're supposed to, I'll look after it. If you decide to stay, do I have your permission to keep it?"

"Yes. Consider the donkey yours from now on. A gift from me. It was my father's wedding gift to me. We'll leave it tied somewhere near the well."

"No, it's not safe out there for a defenceless donkey. Leave it in that small hut and make sure you shut the door. I'll come and get it myself."

"You told us jinn lived in that hut," said Sondus.

"If the donkey belongs to me, the jinn won't come near it," the chief said, laughing. "Very well, you had better get going. Sondus, take this spear in case you encounter a beast. This torch will scare them off and show you the way."

Sondus and the princess took the spear, the torch, and the fetish and said goodbye to the chief, who hurried back to his hut without glancing backwards, muttering a long goodbye.

After the princess mounted the donkey, Sondus took the lead and walked. It was pitch-black and the torch barely cast any light ahead. The villagers gathered somewhere, out of view, intently watching the lovers on their pilgrimage. Sondus and the princess heard the occasional child cry, and the occasional cough followed by hushing. But they kept walking.

The well wasn't close by. It was at least seven miles away, depending on the route one took. There was a shortcut, but it required knowledge and skill. It wasn't clearly marked and was lined with thickets of trees and bushes. For this reason, they avoided it in favour of the longer route, not that the longer route was much easier to traverse. Were it not for the sturdy leather sandals Sondus was wearing, he wouldn't have braved the thorns and sharp dry grass, the insects, scorpions, and venomous spiders. What frightened them most was the eerie howling of the wolves and the snapping of their fangs. They could tell the wolves were far away, but they also knew there were many other predatory animals that hunted silently.

Sondus and the princess were swiftly approaching the well. They were silently pondering their uncertain futures. The princess was still thinking about the God that supposedly resided in a cave. It made no sense to her that a God that had created the whole world in seven days lived in a cave instead of a paradise of his choosing. Even her father, a mere human, had several palaces to his name and thousands of slaves and captives tending to his every need.

There's no turning back now. I'm going with Sondus. But what if the old, blind man was right? Why is Sondus so certain he's not?

Sondus was also preoccupied with God, but the God he waited to meet dwelt in caves. He was a God that restored what humans had lost on earth. A God within reach. Sondus had the fetish that would protect him from danger. He was so close to getting what he wanted, so close to marrying the princess, with or without her father's blessings.

She belongs to me.

They reached the well. Its large, dark opening produced a whistling sound that grew louder as the wind intensified. They could also hear insect sounds emanating from its depths. A pungent smell similar to bat urine wafted up. By the light of the torch, they could see the giant iron ladder hanging on the well. Vines covered the walls, seeking light and fresh air.

The princess dismounted from the donkey holding the fetish in her hands. "Are we taking the donkey in there?" she said, pointing to the hut.

"No, we're going to the coast," said Sondus, bringing the torch closer to her face so he could see it more clearly. "We might find a boat to take us to Pemba. After that we'll go to Mombasa. I think the old man was right. They're coming for us, flying through the dark like bats. They're still miles away but I can feel their breath. I can hear their footsteps in my heart."

"If they mean us harm they'll catch up with us sooner or later. They'll throw us into the well. We'll never make it. Like the old man said, the singer won't rest until she sees us dead," the princess said.

"Let's set fire to the well. They'll see the smoke and think we climbed in. Come on, grab some sturdy wood from the hut."

"What about the donkey?" the princess asked, her heart pounding.

Sondus led the donkey to the hut. "We'll leave it here. Then they'll be sure we went down the well. Travelling with the donkey is easier, but we'd better not. Your shoes are strong like mine. If you get tired I'll carry you. Let's hurry."

Shortly afterwards, the villagers were hurling hefty rocks and tree branches into the well. They moved to the rhythm of drums that echoed through the night, reaching Sondus and the princess and startling the spotted hyenas, which silently retreated into the deep forests. The singer felt utmost delight and triumph, singing:

> If they find God in the distant caves
> And defeat the demon hound
> If they take back their organs
> May their bodies never be found

> Let them stay with the God forevermore
> And the Lord give them bodies truly impure
> For corrupting our village
> For corrupting our sons

> Woe unto us
> If we don't throw more stones
> If we wipe away their sin
> If they don't vanish within

> Woe unto us
> If we slaughter fowl nor goat
> Woe unto us
> If our drums are weak in throat

> If our drums are weak in throat
> And the Lord doesn't hear
> From the depths of his cave
> Their return we must fear
>
> Their blood is the sacrifice
> Their flesh vultures' delight
> The wind will spread their ashes
> Far and wide.

The villagers regarded the singer's improvisation as divine inspiration, and she spared no effort to embed this belief in them. She concluded her song as she always did.

"My people, God has spoken through me. The words of the Almighty were uttered by my small voice, by my mouth that is your mouth. Here is the prophecy coming true before your eyes, and the deadly eagles will leave, never to return. We have atoned for the sins of the sinners with their own blood."

And when the donkey brayed in the hut, it sent everyone fleeing towards the village, abandoning their drums on the ground and their shoes wherever they happened to fall. Their songs and chants, their cries for help and quiet prayers dissipated in the vast, dark emptiness.

MWANA WA IMBOWA

When facing the unknown, love is the only thing that illuminates the path forward. They had no choice but to go on. Silently, holding hands, they walked briskly, taking the path the old man had described. As darkness fell, they stayed on course with the help of a lone star. Immense dangers lurked on the way: snake and wolf dens, jagged cliffs, and steep valleys. Sondus was confident they would make it. The princess, on the other hand, felt that death was closing in from every direction.

They walked for nearly an hour, until the sound of waves and the rise in humidity told them they were near the ocean.

"Let's rest for a moment," the princess said.

They sat on an enormous tree trunk. The princess lay her head on his shoulder, and her body grew heavy. Sondus felt her love flow through his veins. He couldn't express how he felt about her in words. He failed every time he tried. He could only show it with actions: his hand interlocking with hers for warmth, his breath mixing with hers and with the breeze of the ocean, his readiness to die for her. He loved her without words, outside of language, with his whole body. Her love made him feel he could survive the horrors of his strange existence.

She understood all that, and she loved him silently, in her own way. Her upbringing, so detached from ordinary life; her religious education that had been a litany of commands and prohibitions, and texts memorised but not understood; and being the only daughter of a sultan who possessed everything – all of this had moulded her into a taker who never gave. It never crossed her mind that she should express her love to him verbally, because she simply didn't know how to, or perhaps because she was unable to distinguish between his duty as a slave and his actions as a lover.

With the help of his torch, Sondus kept away pests and mosquitoes. But the flame accidentally caught on the dry grass, and their attempts to put out the fire failed. All the princess's fears were unleashed at once: the darkness, the wild beasts, the villagers, the curse that pursued the man she loved. She began to scream. Sondus did everything he could to bring her and the fire under control. He screamed at her to bring her back to her senses. When she fell silent, the flames also retreated.

They sat silently, their hearts pounding. She placed her head on his lap and eventually fell asleep. He was exhausted but resisted closing her eyes, listening for sounds and deciphering them. Some were from animals he recognised, others he didn't. His imagination painted pictures of fangs and claws. Then he heard the sound of slow but steady footsteps. They started and stopped. He gripped his spear and tapped the princess's shoulder softly. There were still embers burning and smoke rising from small pieces of wood. "Wake up," he whispered.

The princess startled awake, but he held her down with one hand while holding the spear in the other.

"Shh. I hear footsteps. Put your back to the tree and stay still."

She clung tightly to his back as if trying to immerse herself in his flesh, trembling like a leaf. A bout of crying and wailing seized her, and she didn't stop until a voice emerged from the darkness. "Jambo," it said gently. "Remember me?"

The princess poked her head from the side of Sondus's broad back. "Mwana wa Imbowa!" she said.

His laugh rang out like the bark of a dog. "Yes, it's me."

The princess sighed and let Sondus go, laughing nervously. "You scared me! I almost pissed myself."

Mwana wa Imbowa was the one who had led them out of Unguja. They had later come across him in the village assembly, and many other times in the village. He stood out because of his large frame, and was perhaps the tallest among the men. By far the most memorable thing about him in Sondus's mind was what he had said in the village assembly, which had struck Sondus as evil. He was arguing in favour of treating others as they treated you. Thanks to an adage passed down generations – "Evil cannot be fought with evil" – that hadn't come to pass.

The man rested on his spear, whose blade he had dug into the ground.

"I've been following you all the way from the village, but I kept my distance. Then I lost track of you when you took a different route from the well. I fell for your trick and thought you had fallen in and died, or you had met God, if it's true that he lives in the well. But when I inspected the well, I found no trace of you. The sound of braying coming from the haunted hut scared me half to death. But I didn't run away and soon realised it was just the donkey. That's when I realised you had left it there to make us think you had climbed into the well. What you should have done was to leave it tied nearby so everyone would see it. Or take it with you. After all, no one needed convincing that you would go down the well. It was what the singer said would happen. She said she could see your funeral as clear as day, that she could touch your blood with her fingertips.

"As my people approached with drums and their hearts full of rage, I followed you. It wasn't easy. It was dark, and I knew you didn't know your way around. My maternal grandfather had described the route, so I knew where to go. Remember the old, blind man and his brother who is hard of hearing? They're the ones who told me to come and find you. And once I found you – if you hadn't gone down the well – they instructed me to take you to the coast and find a boat to take you to Pemba. They really didn't want anything terrible to happen to you, those kind old men.

"When I couldn't find you along the route I know like the back of my hand, I knew you were lost. I was beginning to lose hope, until you lit a fire. I followed the smell. This is one of my gifts – my nose is as keen as a hunting dog's. Then I heard the princess scream, because my hearing too is as sharp as a dog's."

He squatted and released his axe from the leather pouch around his waist.

"I brought you milk, dried meat, and wine. If you don't drink wine, I can drink it. You must be starving. When we reach the ocean, we can fish. I have a fishing rod and good bait. These are the things a man ought never to leave his home without: his axe, his fishing rod, his pocketknife, and his courage."

"I prefer milk, but she'll drink a little wine. It'll calm her nerves," said Sondus.

"All I need is for us to get back safely to Unguja. I can't take this anymore. I want to rest. I want to sleep for long hours and not worry. I want to talk to my father. How far is Pemba from Unguja?"

"Don't you know where you are? You're by Yabimwa Wana village. If you walk for thirty minutes you'll find yourself there. And you'll immediately be killed. All the surrounding villages know your story. In the morning they'll be satisfied to know you're buried in the ground or among the spirits in the sky. If they see you, they'll simply think you're ghosts. You should be thankful I caught up with you, or your life would have become much more complicated.

You'd probably have never seen your father again. I know what that feels like. My parents were killed by the slavers," Mwana said.

"My people are barbaric," offered the princess apologetically.

"All humans are barbaric. Only animals know what compassion is," he replied. His voice was soft and steady.

They proceeded to grill meat strips. Mwana rekindled the fire, adding twigs and leaves and tapping them with the blade of his axe.

"Won't the smell attract the animals?" asked Sondus.

"The smell of roasted meat scares them. It tells them there is a vicious predator, a skilful hunter, nearby. It's the smell of blood that awakens their hunger, because it means there's prey. An animal knows very well who its predator is and who its prey is. Just as humans do." He laughed.

Is that why they call him Son of a Bitch? Because of his laugh? thought the princess.

The food was delicious, the night calm and serene. A few bright stars appeared in the sky as it became clearer. A soft breeze blew from the east. The vicious mosquitoes sang a riotous song. It brought Sondus and the princess boundless comfort to be in the company of such a strong and courageous man who knew the land and all its secrets. Even the cries of the hyenas no longer affected them. The wine left the princess a little lighter, a little bolder. She was suddenly able to recall an Arabic song performed by her father's band. She didn't understand all the lyrics, so naturally she knew nothing about the person who had written it, a Sufi poet called Mansur al-Hallaj. She started to hum it softly:

> O breeze, carry my plea
> Tell the fawn about the yearning in me
> Even the spring can't quench my thirst
> My love runs so deep my heart could burst
> If my lover wished, I would let her stroll
> Along my cheeks, to merge with my soul.

Their laughter filled the air. Only Sondus abstained from drinking. In the service of the princess, he had to stay alert and avoid excess in all its forms: fullness, hunger, joy, sorrow. She, on the other hand, could be as excessive as she pleased. She loved to drink to the point of near oblivion. Sondus would then have to carry her back to her room, replace her evening dress with her nightgown, and lay her in bed on her ostrich-feather pillow. He would sleep on a mat by her bed. When she needed the bathroom at night, he would bring the receptacle and help her sit on it. He would lift her gown and gently spread her legs. He would wait until she stopped dripping, then pour warm water between her legs with his right hand, and wipe her with his left, and dry her with a cotton towel before carrying her back to her bed. He would rub her back until her breath became soft and steady. Then he would go back to his mat and sleep with one eye open.

The princess fell asleep on Sondus's lap while he had his back to the tree. Mwana passed out next to the ash. His snores blared like the horns of a British warship scouring the ocean. He dreamt of his mother, the dog that belonged to his grandfather, as he did every night.

THE BOAT

On the coast, in the early morning, the princess recalled her towering palace, the balcony that overlooked the endless ocean interrupted only by enormous ships, flocks of seagulls, and winter's colossal, roaring waves. Overwhelmed with a deep longing, she ran onto the sand like a child. She sat on a small rock and started to wash her body, humming Swahili songs from her childhood. Every so often, she would sigh aloud: "How I miss you, Unguja."

Sondus and Mwana wa Imbowa, meanwhile, were cutting a tree branch to construct a boat that would take them to Pemba. The sight of the ocean brought back memories to Sondus about the day he had been captured and transported on a slave boat. The same rope bound him and his father by the neck. The ocean was still. Flying fish leapt out of the water, hovering, and then plunged back in. Seagulls sat on the perch, their screeching filling the air. Aboard the boat had been twenty captives; four black men armed with spearlike weapons that could shoot fire, poised for action;

and a slaver who had one of the same spears, as well as a whip made of hippopotamus hide, which he never hesitated to use on the bare backs of captives. Sondus had received his share of searing lashes. He had never experienced anything like it, but he'd remained as silent as the older captives whipped before him. All he could think about was what awaited them once the boat arrived. People in his village had been talking about a far more severe punishment the slavers inflicted on men. It left them unable to bear children or even urinate unless they squatted like women. They said slavers came to see them as women and did with them as they pleased.

Mwana wa Imbowa didn't let Sondus drift all the way into his grief. He talked constantly as he chopped the wood, about revolution and the inevitable changes that awaited Unguja and the African mainland. He talked about taking up arms, now and then repeating the phrase "We will not forgive." He talked about a group of religious men who visited the village from time to time, inviting people into the religion the Portuguese had brought with them many years prior. But word had spread that anyone who followed this faith turned as wicked as the Portuguese.

"My grandfather once said to them, 'A tree is identifiable by its fruit.' Their answer was that faith cannot be wicked, only man can. But my grandfather told them about another group of white people on the mainland who followed the same faith and talked about tolerance, compassion, and forgiveness, yet they didn't hesitate to murder Africans. Their only concern was acquiring diamonds, gold, and a viscous substance extracted from certain trees. They ordered the locals to work for them for no pay, indefinitely, and if they refused their hands and feet would be severed. They called them Belgians. No, we will not forgive. We have guns, but not nearly enough. What we have enough of is people. And that trumps any quantity of guns. We have the determination. I, for one, have all the rage I need to defeat them, and a great urge for revenge. My mother visits me in all my dreams to ask how I can sleep at night.

Sondus, accustomed to a lifetime of silence, didn't say much, but he listened closely. The news about the sultan was tremendous if it meant an end to slavery, but Sondus couldn't entertain the idea that Africans would one day rule their own lands. He knew that the sultan's power and evil were limitless. He would one day rise and defeat the British, just as the Arabs had once fought the Portuguese and tossed their bodies into the ocean. He had to see the sultan with his own eyes to believe the things he'd heard. How could anyone have made the sultan a eunuch? God himself couldn't have. Neither could any sorcerer. The sultan was the most powerful sorcerer of them all. And he had an army of jinn serving him.

Mwana and Sondus took some time to fish and eat, and the rest of their time was spent telling stories and working on the small boat made of young mahogany. It was arduous work, especially the chopping, but Mwana firmly believed that if you couldn't complete a piece of work with a handful of tools, you couldn't complete it with a large number of tools either.

"Do you know the singer Uhuru?"

"Yes." The princess was engrossed in a losing battle trying to remove bones from the fish. "I love her, even though she's shameless. She shows the whole world her naked body," she added.

Mwana burst out laughing.

"The princess always took me to see her in the market. But only from a distance," said Sondus. "They say she gathered all the elderly people who had been abandoned on Unguja's coast by a mysterious ship. They were sickly and starving, so she took them to live with her. That's what the guards said."

Mwana placed a huge chunk of fish in his mouth without removing the bone.

"Her father was a great man. She's a queen, a daughter and granddaughter of kings," said Mwana.

"When we get back to Unguja, we'll take care of her and the people she took in," said the princess. She was staring at the horizon as though expecting Uhuru to emerge.

Calm as ever, Mwana said, "Isn't Mombasa better for you two?"

"No. I want to see my father. Unguja is my home. It's where I want to live with Sondus. We'll marry in Unguja. We'll be together forever."

Mwana was silent for a while, then he ate the final piece of fish. He told Sondus to get back to the work, which was nearing completion, and asked the princess to try catching another fish.

Later Mwana said to Sondus, "You know, you're a strong man, Sondus. You have to protect your freedom and think seriously about revenge, or you'll always be as you are now. No God can give you back your manhood. Only you can get it back. The boat is almost ready, and once it's finished, we may not see each other again. If you want to be free, you have to decide to seek out your freedom."

Sondus was quiet for a few seconds before replying. "But I am free."

Mwana climbed into the boat and sat. "Freedom doesn't mean being out of your master's reach. It means *being* the master. This can't happen without making sacrifices, serious sacrifices. What I mean is that you must get rid of everything that weighs you down, including the princess."

"But she's part of me. She's my freedom. The princess and I are one."

"I know it was because of her that you forgave her father for what he did to you and your father and your people. This is how someone might think if they're under the spell of slavery. Their minds can't think straight. The murdered don't forgive, Sondus. Their souls can find no peace until their killers receive their due. But I understand you. I just hope you remember what I'm telling you when you get to Unguja. If you decide you want revolution, there are people you should seek out. You've never met them, but you know them. Try to find them. Look, the boat is now ready."

"Thank you for all your help."

"I have high hopes that you'll learn a lot, and that you'll work to help your people. That's why I built you this boat. I built it especially for you."

"Asante sana."

"Karibu."

The princess didn't succeed in catching another fish. She didn't really try. Her father had told her that her mother had died because she had hunted an elephant, the last in Unguja. She had shot her with a rifle.

Then the elephant's soul came back and bore down on your mother's chest until she suffocated to death.

The boat was only large enough for two people, but the distance to the island was a mere two miles. Mwana offered to navigate the boat twice. He told them to choose who would go first.

"One of you can wait here. It's safe. You'll be fine. The boat is small, and it requires some skill to keep from toppling. Besides, neither of you can swim. You'll drown like two big stones and disappear into the ocean's belly. When you get to Pemba, you'll find a group of fishermen who will take you to Unguja. What do you say?"

"Are the fishermen waiting on the island as we speak?" asked the princess.

"Yes. There are always a few at least."

"In that case, take Sondus first. I'd rather wait here. You know what fishermen are like. They're the same way as seamen."

Mwana laughed. "The real danger is the pythons found all over that island. In any case, let's go. This is a good plan. The ocean is calm and there's no wind. It won't take us long to get across. "And you, stay where you are," he said to the princess. "Don't go into the jungle, no matter what. The animals from the jungle won't come this far. They don't drink seawater. And the birds are harmless, as you know. The villagers never come here either. This coast has been deserted for a long time. I'll leave my two spears and my axe here. I'll be back to fetch you as soon as possible."

THE STORY OF THE DOG

As the boat inched closer to the princess on the coast, she frantically waved her hands, and then the spears and the axe. She was so happy she could have taken flight. It hadn't taken the boat long to return, yet she had been riddled with anxiety, clutching onto the spear, ready to battle the unknown. She had anticipated that it would emerge from the ocean, between the trees in the jungle, from the sky above, or that it would erupt from the ground like a volcano.

The ocean stretched before her like a carpet cut out of the blue sky. She adored the ocean, but only from a distance. She loved the seamen's songs and strange tales, but only if she heard them through someone else. She was the kind of person who preferred there to be a vast distance separating her from life, the kind of person for whom it's enough to smell the fragrance of a garden rather than spend time in it, for whom the sound of waves is preferable to being near the ocean, and for whom the rustle of the seagulls' wings is beautiful only when it's far away – the kind of person who preferred to live behind a sheet of glass.

Mwana's body was drenched. The princess helped him anchor the boat. It was barely a boat; it was a tree trunk with a carved-out centre. People on Pemba and Unguja only used boats like these when there was no other recourse. They favoured the local tishtari boats, which were easy enough to construct if the materials were available: dry wood and plenty of time. To maintain balance, Mwana had tied two large, dry branches to the side of the boat, using a rope he had fashioned from palm fronds with Sondus's help. Mwana wa Imbowa was drenched because he'd had to jump into the water to save Sondus, who had fallen in twice. He hadn't been able to keep himself from turning his body to find the princess in the distance, even though Mwana had repeatedly told him not to do so.

The princess was ready to climb into the boat, but Mwana asked to rest for a moment. "Sondus wore me out. He'll play a big role in the revolution, that man. The pain he went through, the pain he is yet to go through – it's enormous. Profound suffering transforms us into great beings."

He threw his fishing rod into the water and caught a small meandering tuna fish in no time, as if the fish were waiting to be snatched. He slammed the handle of his axe onto its head and it went limp. He scaled and gutted it with a pocketknife, placed it on stones that rested atop a fire he had lit, sprinkled some salt, and let it slowly cook.

"Why have you never asked me why they call me Son of a Bitch?" Mwana asked calmly.

"It's because when you laugh you sound like a dog barking," she said with a wide grin. Seeing his surprised expression, she hurried to add, "I'm only joking."

He laughed. "I'll tell you the story now. I told it to Sondus as we crossed to Pemba. I wanted him to know it before we parted ways, but I didn't manage to. I only told him the part that concerned him. The story in its entirety concerns you. It's almost like it's been waiting for you. Or maybe you were waiting for it. I just mean that the story is the reason why you and I met at all. It brought you to me and placed you in my path. Our people say stories have souls. They live and die. They're as powerful as the storm. Should I tell it now or wait until after we eat?"

"I'm excited to hear it, especially if it concerns me."

"Okay," he said, turning the fish and gazing at the hot stone and the delicate white smoke emanating from it. "It happened two weeks after I was born, according to my grandfather and the village elders. The story I'm about to tell you was told to me many times by many different people. Maybe they were afraid I would forget it. I've never repeated it to anyone yet. This will be the first and last time. It began during the yam harvest. My mother, my father, and several relatives were working at our farm. I was placed in a small basket made of palm fronds under a tree with abundant shade. My mother cleared the weeds around me. She was quite young. Maybe sixteen or seventeen years old. I was her first child. My father, too, was about twenty years old."

A pause.

"The truth is, I don't know how to tell you this story."

"However you want. I'm listening."

Mwana flipped the tuna again and placed two hot stones in its gut and smaller stones on the rest of its body.

"To cut a long story short, the slavers attacked and in a matter of seconds captured everyone, as they always do. I escaped their notice, so I wasn't taken. I almost starved to death, but my grandfather's dog found me. She stayed with me and fed me along with her young. She had four puppies. They usually followed my family wherever they went, like all the other village dogs. But what she did for me was extraordinary. She carried me in the basket and took me to the village, to my grandfather's home. My grandfather was the only one in my family who was still alive after the slavers had gone away with his only daughter, my mother. My grandmother had died a few years prior. It was magic that took her, they said. My grandfather asked several mothers in the village to take me and nurse me, but none were willing. They wouldn't let me touch them because I had been fed by a dog. He didn't know what to do. Then he realised the dog was sneaking into my bed to feed me. That came as no surprise to him, as he knew dogs were often far nobler than humans. At the time, my grandfather wasn't yet blind. That happened years later.

"I was brought up with the dog's young. I became strong and was able to consume other food. This happened very quickly. They say I learned to walk within a few months and that my body grew disproportionately to my age. I followed the dog and her young wherever she went. I knew all the dogs in the village – I was one of them. I don't think I ever knew their language, but I do understand them, and they understand me. I listened to their word and they listened to mine. We shared food. I don't know if you'll understand me or not, but I'm not embarrassed to admit that I also had sex with dogs, and there may be offspring of mine somewhere. In any case, my dog mother died, and her young died, but I remained close to the generation that followed. Of course, I was also one of the village's inhabitants, and they respected and feared me. It's true I could be quite violent sometimes, a vicious warrior, but I was never cast away. They understood and respected my relationship with dogs. All of this is to say that I am very loyal to my mother and heartbroken about what happened to her. Do you want to know what happened to her?"

The princess's gaze was fixed on him.

"It was your father. He raped her. The slavers captured her. He selected her out of all the women. Her body was still weak because she went back to work soon after giving birth to me. People say she lost a lot of blood. Everyone knows your father has a hyena's prick. My mother died under the weight of his massive body. Then he ordered for her to be taken away and buried."

"I – I'm sorry. My father was a criminal," said the princess, fear seizing her.

"Yes, he was a criminal. A murderer," he said as he came

nearer. "My mother did nothing wrong. She did nothing to deserve to die that way."

"You're right."

Mwana began to frantically flick sand onto the fish.

"She always visits me in my dreams asking me to avenge her. And it looks like the time has come. I'm going to do to you what your father did to my mother. I have been thinking about this from the moment Sondus took you from the palace. The day we ransacked it for guns. I knew my mother's soul would rest because of you. You yourself did nothing wrong. Just like my mother. And I'm like your father, a savage man."

The princess stood up, her body trembling. "I didn't do anything. It was him. I've never killed a living being. Kill my father. He deserves it. I didn't do anything."

Mwana didn't stir.

"My mother never hurt a living being. She's just like you. That's the point. Your blood will let my mother's soul rest, more so than the blood of a murderer like your father. His blood is not worthy of my mother's. His blood is tainted."

"Blood is blood. Just as water is water," the princess said, trying to stay calm.

"When the storm blows, it uproots the thorny shrub just as it uproots the clove tree. Your father and I are nothing but thorny trees, while you and my mother are clove trees. All of us, good or evil, are destined to be swept up by the storm."

Mwana stood up and, like an eagle, swooped down on her. His large, rough hand snatched hers, cold as if drained of blood, as if seawater ran through her veins. She fainted and fell onto his shoulder. He lay her softly on the sand while the seagulls cried loudly from the small boat. With quick steps, he released the boat into the waves and watched it drift away, while the seagulls perched on it like bewitched, feathered pirates sailing into nothingness. He stopped to catch his breath. He took his axe and tossed it in the direction of the jungle. It sank into the sand. He turned to the ocean, took one of his spears, and threw it into the water. The second spear he threw into the sky above. It flew in the air and fell back into the sand, its blade sinking in, not too far from where he stood. His heart was pounding. His blood was simmering like the waves in a violent storm. He carried her with trembling hands and placed her on a small rock by the water. Then he muttered something like a prayer:

> Your blood is my mother's blood
> My mother's blood is your blood
> Your blood is my mother's blood
> My mother's blood is your blood

"Forgive me, Grandfather, for deceiving you. Forgive me, Sondus, for deceiving you. Forgive me, my heart. I will show no mercy. My mother's soul is waiting for me. The murdered don't forgive. Their souls will find no rest if a blood offering is not made. Forgive me. I had no choice. Your father left me without a choice. My redemption is your redemption.

Only your blood is worthy of my mother's blood. If this isn't God's justice, it's Satan's injustice. I'm the deliverer of them both."

Then he screamed at the top of his voice, "Samahani."

EVIL INSIDE THE HUMAN'S HEART

Sondus knew something strange was happening to the princess. His heart told him. Time was ticking very slowly as he watched the horizon, waiting for the boat to appear. From where he stood, the other coast was a dark mass, the trees large, black stones. He stood waiting for an agonising hour. Finally, he went to one of the fishermen and asked him to take him to the other side. "I'll give you these gold earrings."

The fisherman studied the earrings in his palm. He sniffed them. Then he tied them to the edge of his turban. "This is more than the price of the trip," he said with a smile as brown as tobacco. "But I need it to finish paying for my wedding. I prayed and prayed for Allah's help, and he sent you to me. As our prophet Mohammed said, "Allah doesn't forget his servants." If Allah wills it he can send a fisherman a pair of gold earrings all the way from a faraway island. Shawiri ya Mawjudu." He looked at the other coast and added, "Bismillah. Get in. It will take us about an hour."

As they approached the coast, a naked body lying on a rock came into view. Near it, another body. As they inched closer, Sondus saw it was the princess on the rock, and the other body was a giant doglike animal, like the one the village chief had described, the hound that guards God's caves. It lay serenely next to her, as if in a deep slumber. As Sondus lay his feet on the sand with the fisherman's help, it became clear what had occurred. "The dog," he cried out with all his might.

The dog stirred. He regarded them with tired, reddened eyes. Then he scattered, barking, towards the jungle.

"I know that dog," the fisherman said, trembling in fear. "I know that dog. It's the dog from the cursed well! God's well!"

Sondus ran towards the princess. "You *don't* know him," he said bitterly. "He is evil itself. Evil that dwells in a human's heart."

Sondus's trembling fingers touched the princess's cold body. There was dried blood in her nostrils, the bite marks of a dog on her lips and chest, and remnants of fur all over her body. Between her thighs, a thread of dried blood mixed with a fluid coagulated like curdled milk.

In history, as in nature, decay is the laboratory of life.

KARL MARX

Foundry Editions
40 Randolph Street
London NW1 0SR
United Kingdom

Copyright © Abdelaziz Baraka Sakin 2017

First published in 2017 as سماهاني by Masciliana Editions, Tunis

Translation © Mayada Ibrahim and Adil Babakir 2024

This first edition published by Foundry Editions in 2024

The moral right of Abdelaziz Baraka Sakin to be identified as the Author of this work has been asserted in accordance with the Copyright, Designs and Patents Act 1988

A CIP record for this title is available from the British Library

ISBN 978-1-7384463-6-0

Series cover design by Murmurs Design
Designed and typeset in LfA Aluminia by Tetragon, London
ARC Printed and bound by CPI Group (UK) Ltd

All rights reserved. No part of this publication may be reproduced, stored in a retrieval system or transmitted in any form or by any means, electronic, mechanical, photocopying, recording or otherwise, without prior permission in writing from Foundry Editions.

foundryeditions.co.uk

FOR ALL PRESS ENQUIRIES,
PLEASE CONTACT MIDAS PR

ANNA ZANETTI — anna.zanetti@midaspr.co.uk
EMILY LAIDLAW — emily.laidlaw@midaspr.co.uk

FOR ALL SALES ENQUIRIES,
PLEASE CONTACT INPRESS BOOKS

London & the South East

KATE ELLIS — kate@inpressbooks.co.uk

The North

JAMES BENSON — jamesbenson@btinternet.com

Wales, the South West & East Anglia

IAN TRIPP — iantripp@ymail.com

Scotland

DON MORRISON — donmoleith@gmail.com

Ireland

GEOFF BRYAN — independentpublishersagent@gmail.com

Key Accounts & National Retailers

JANE PIKE — jane@inpressbooks.co.uk

FOUNDRY EDITIONS

CONSTANTIA SOTERIOU
Brandy Sour

Translation by Lina Protopapa

CYPRUS

When it was built in the 1950s, nothing symbolised Cyprus entering the modern world like the Ledra Palace Hotel. In Constantia Soteriou's jewel of a novel, the ambitions and shortcomings of the island's turbulent twentieth century are played out by its occupants. Among them we meet the king in exile who needs to drown his sorrows with a drink disguised to look like tea; the porter who, amidst the English roses of the hotel's gardens, secretly plants a rose from his village to make his rosebud infusions with; the UN officer who drinks lemonade to deal with the heat and the lies; and the cleaning lady who always carries her holy water with her. They are reluctant actors in history, evocatively captured in this moving, personal, and highly original portrait of civil strife and division.

Brandy Sour won the 2023 National Book Prize in Cyprus and Constantia Soteriou won the 2019 Commonwealth Short Story Prize.

MARIA GRAZIA CALANDRONE
Your Little Matter
Translation by Antonella Lettieri
ITALY

Rome, 1965. A man and a woman, excluded from Italian society, abandon their eight-month-old daughter in the Villa Borghese and take extreme action. In 2021, that child, author Maria Grazia Calandrone, sets out to discover the truth about what happened, examining the places where her mother lived, suffered, worked, and loved.

Your Little Matter is a reconstruction of the life and death of a parent, a shocking insight into the real lives of marginalised women from the Italian South, and the examination of a cause célèbre that was a catalyst for social change in Italy. Combining poetic insight with journalistic investigation, the personal and the public, the book tells a devastating story of how the institutionalised callousness of state and society can lead to tragedy.

Your Little Matter was shortlisted for the 2023 Premio Strega.

FOUNDRY EDITIONS

1   CONSTANTIA SOTERIOU (CYPRUS)
Brandy Sour
tr. from Greek by Lina Protopapa

2   MARIA GRAZIA CALANDRONE (ITALY)
Your Little Matter
tr. from Italian by Antonella Lettieri

3   ROSA RIBAS (SPAIN)
Far
tr. from Spanish by Charlotte Coombe

4   ABDELAZIZ BARAKA SAKIN (SUDAN)
Samahani
tr. from Arabic by Mayada Ibrahim and Adil Babikir

5   ESTHER GARCÍA LLOVET (SPAIN)
Spanish Beauty
tr. from Spanish by Richard Village

6   KARIM KATTAN (PALESTINE)
The Palace on Two Hills
tr. from French by Jeffrey Zuckerman

7   ANNA PAZOS (SPAIN)
Killing the Nerve
tr. from Catalan by Laura McGloughlin and Charlotte Coombe